Seven fo.
never tc

A Ghost Story for Children

Joy McNally-Bells

Isbn-13:978-1542 976343
Isbn-10:1542976340

Dedication

For Natasha who lights up the darkest corners

Acknowledgments

Love and thanks to Robin Hanley who encouraged me to write and gave me valuable time and sound advice. Thank you to Glenn Parsons (a.k.a. Uncle Animal) for his proof reading skills. Also a big thank you to Joshua Clarke and Ava Robinson for their help with draft reading and suggestions.

1

Christmas Eve
1950

Snow is falling. Swirling specks of white dance through the icy air. The heavy, red sun sinks below a dark horizon and the sky is injected with the inky blue of impending night. Sirius the bright winter star twinkles like a fabulous jewel and distant carol singing can be heard coming from the church on the hill a mile away.

All this is lost to the six boys walking across the open field. Tomorrow is Christmas day and they talk about the presents they hope to unwrap, how much they will eat and whether they will sneak a swig of beer when everyone is falling asleep during the King's speech on the radio. Suddenly out of the darkness behind them a voice shouts.

'Help me. Help me.'

They are momentarily silent then stifle involuntary giggles. A moment later a more distressed scream rips through the air. The boys don't giggle this time. The boys keep walking and the snow keeps falling until eventually the boys leave the field. Their footsteps in the snow are covered with new snow and it's as if they'd never been there.

2

The Present Day

'Are you awake?' Mia's Nan called up the stairs. Mia didn't answer. She was looking out of her bedroom window. She was watching a magpie. It was perched on the large wooden gates at the end of the back garden preening it's long, black tail feathers. The gates were bigger than Mia and bigger than her Nan who had to stand on tip toe to slide the top bolt to open them. There were three sets of bolts. 'These gates are great for making sure the dog doesn't get out,' Mia's Nan had said when they moved there. Mia thought they were great for making sure 'something' didn't get in.

Mia's Nan came into Mia's bedroom with her school boots. She walked to the window and looked out.

'One's for sorrow,' she said. Mia gave her a quizzical look. 'The magpie. There's an old rhyme about them, it goes, one for sorrow, two for joy, three for a girl, four for a boy, five for silver, six for gold, seven for a secret never to be told.'

'Why's one for sorrow?' asked Mia.

'I always think it's because you usually see two or more together. If you only see one it means he's lost his friends. He's all by himself in the world. There's a lot of magpies around here. Maybe that's why our cottage is called Magpie Cottage.' Mia's Nan made a pretend stern face. 'Now, get dressed or you'll be late for school.'

Mia looked out beyond the back gates into the field behind the cottage. A thin mist hung above the long grass. Inside she felt a heavy ache and wished her mum was there. She shook off the sensation. Her mum would be back by the summer holidays she told herself. Until then she'd just have to get on with it.

Mia brushed her long hair. Today it was a soft, warm brown, but sometimes it seemed red, sometimes gold depending on the light. She pulled it into a tight sideways pony tail, then checked it in the mirror and smiled at the result.

As she pulled on her boots she remembered something from last night. She'd woken up, her room was in complete darkness and then she heard the sound of someone crying. It seemed a long way away. Outside somewhere. Then she drifted off to sleep again. Over breakfast she told her Nan about the crying but her Nan said she was dreaming.

'It could have been anything Mia, the wind, cats meowing. Me snoring! Now wash your hands and go and get your bike, I'll be out in a minute.' Mia thought that if her Nan had heard the crying she would have believed her.

She left her Nan in the bathroom and went to the larder and quickly stuffed a packet of crisps into her bag before making her way up the garden to take her bike out of the shed. Mia and her Nan cycled to school along a bumpy, cobbled path and across the playing field. Her Nan left her at the school gate and carried on to the shops. The school bus was pulling in bringing children from the outlying villages and Mia stopped to wait for Safi.

She didn't remember how their friendship began. Safi had come from Iraq with his family a few years ago. His dad had been an interpreter for the British army during a war that had happened before both Mia and Safi were born. Safi was a quick thinker, he was the only boy in year 6 that instantly knew the answer to any random multiplication the teacher threw at him. He had curly, jet-black hair and big, bright eyes and even though he was always eating he was the smallest boy in his class. Mia was the total opposite. She hated maths. Her favourite things were drawing, dancing and making up stories. She was one of the tallest girls in school with pale blue eyes and freckles across her nose…but in spite of their differences she and Safi were best friends.

The biggest thing they had in common was a TV program called Warriors of Albion. They loved it. They made up games around the characters and joined the Warriors of Albion fan club. They had posters, books, stationary and anything they could get their hands on that had a Warriors of Albion theme.

The other thing that made them feel connected was that Mia's mum was in the army and had been in Iraq during the difficult times of the war and had known Safi's mum and dad. Whatever it was, they hit it off straight away back in year 4 when Safi first came to Evercombe primary.

'Hey, you look like the dog's eaten your breakfast,' Safi rolled his eyes at Mia's words.

'I haven't got a dog!' he said '…and if I did I would have given him my breakfast.' Mia laughed.

'Eggs again?' she said, stopping and opening her back pack. 'There you go.' she handed him the packet of crisps she'd sneaked into her bag.

'You've saved my life!' he announced dramatically, tearing into the foil and stuffing several crisps into his mouth at once. Mia put her bike in the bike shed. 'Did you watch Warriors of Albion last night?' Safi asked excitedly.

'Of course. I just want them to rescue the Thistle Magician, he's been a prisoner of the Witch of Sardeeni for five weeks. Five weeks!'

'Well I think when King Constantine comes back from the North Kingdom he'll be rescued.' He opened the top of the crisp packet, tipped back his head and poured the last little crispy bits into his mouth. The bell rang to line up. 'See y'later and thanks for the crisps.' Mia smiled and joined her queue.

3

At lunch time Mia and Safi played Warriors of Albion and decided they'd rescue the Thistle Magician without waiting for next week's episode. They couldn't stop laughing when Jake, who was playing with them kept saying the Witch of sardines instead of Sardeeni.

Time went quickly and when the bell rang at the end of the day Mia hurried out to meet her Nan and Bear her dog at the school gate. Bear jumped up and nibbled her sleeve.

That night it was the history group meeting. Mia's Nan held the meetings in her cottage and the members came to talk about people who used to live in the village a long time ago. They found out things about the manor house and the church and looked at old maps and photographs. Mia liked the history group night because her Nan let her have a pot noodle with thick slices of buttered bread for tea. Tonight it was barbeque beef flavour. Mia's favourite.

Mia's jobs on the night of the history group meeting were to put the cups on a tray and arrange biscuits on a willow patterned plate ready for when everybody wanted a cup of tea or coffee. Mia's Nan had bought jaffa cakes and chocolate digestives. Mia ate a digestive with her glass of milk before bed. Bed time was always early when it was history group night and Bear who wasn't allowed upstairs was confined to the utility room.

Mia's Nan's cottage had two small downstairs rooms and members of the group would gather in the back room next to the kitchen. They sat around the old oak dining table on an assortment of mismatched chairs and stools. The stairs went up from this back room and Mia would sit on the top step unseen. She liked to listen to everyone talking. There was Tommy Jones the retired vet and his wife. John from the bowls club, Sam who lived at the end cottage and Paul Gregory one of the teachers from Evercombe Academy. Not everyone came every week. Mrs Hewitt who investigated family histories wasn't there and Robin, the history student from college was on holiday.

Miss Jaggers was there. Mia liked Miss Jaggers. She was quite a bit older than Mia's Nan and had dyed orange hair, red varnished fingernails and a loud laugh that came out quick like a bark. She was born in the village and was always telling stories about the 'old days'. They were just talking about the back garden and Mia's Nan was saying she'd lost her ring while she was digging broken bricks out of the flower beds.

'You'll find a lot of bricks out there. That field out the back of your cottage was the old brick works Meg,' Miss Jaggers told Mia's Nan. 'They dug up so much clay to make bricks it left a great big hole, then when the war started the brick works was abandoned. That big hole filled up with water and it didn't drain away so there was a permanent lake out there. When I was a nipper every sunny day of the summer holidays we'd be swimming in it and every winter it would ice over and we'd be skating.'

'Where's the lake now then?' asked Mia's Nan. Sam who lived at the end cottage answered.

'It was used for waste. Bottles, wood and ashes. Back in the sixties. You'd never know now because it's all grown over.' Mrs Jones, who very rarely said anything added softly.

'But wasn't there a boy who…'

'Mia page!' Mia's Nan was peering up the stairs. 'Into bed.'

'Can I have a drink of water please?' asked Mia. Her Nan smiled and gave her a wink. 'Get into bed and I'll bring it up.'

Mia reluctantly got into bed and minutes later her Nan was there with a glass of water.

'What was Mrs Jones saying…about a boy?' Her Nan gave her a kiss.

'I'll ask her when I get the chance. Mr Gregory's going to give us a talk about Evercombe in Roman times first.' She walked out of the room and whispered *sweet dreams*.

Mia curled up on her left side. Her Nan had told her that East was in that direction. East of England was Germany and her mum was in Germany. '*Love you mum,*' she whispered.

4

Friday was swimming day at school and Mia couldn't find her swimming costume. She'd looked everywhere.

'I'm sure I washed it and left it on the back of the chair in your bedroom,' Mia's Nan said rummaging through the wash basket. 'It's not here either. Look, I'd better get the bikes out or you'll be late, run upstairs and get your old one from the suitcase under my bed…it'll fit at a stretch. Just till yours turns up.'

Mia ran upstairs into her Nan's bedroom and pulled the suitcase from under the bed. She looked quickly through the old clothes inside but her attention was caught by a sound. It was a slow tapping sound. She looked up trying to work out where it was coming from. It was outside her Nan's bedroom. She went onto the landing where she could hear the sound more clearly. Tap….tap….tap. It was coming from her own room. She gently pushed open her bedroom door.

The tap….tap….tap continued and she saw that it was actually a drip…drip…drip. Her swimming costume was exactly where her Nan had said it would be on the back of her chair. Mia was confused. It hadn't been there earlier. She walked over and picked it up. It was soaking wet. It had been dripping onto her bedroom floor and had left a small puddle.

'Have you found it?' her Nan called up the stairs.

'I've found my proper swimsuit!' Mia shouted, 'but it's still wet. It's still *really* wet!'

'You must have spilt something on it. Now get a move on or you'll be late.' Mia went back to the suitcase and found her old swimming costume, wrapped it in a towel and put it in her bag. She brought the wet one down stairs to show her Nan. 'Well it was dry when I put it there,' her Nan said. Mia sighed.

'…and it wasn't on the chair earlier either. I looked. I looked properly.'

'I'm sure there's a rational explanation. I'll try and think back,' said Mia's Nan. 'Maybe I didn't dry it... you know what I'm like trying to do half a dozen things at once.'

Mia felt uneasy. Even if her Nan had left it there after she'd pulled it out of the washing machine without drying it, it would never have been wet enough to be dripping on the floorboards. And another thing. Last night she had definitely heard someone crying again.

5

Mia was happy it was Friday. It had been a cold, dark winter but now the evenings were getting lighter and today the sun was shining. Safi was coming to tea after school which meant they could take Bear to play in the field behind Mia's house.

Mia waited outside Safi's classroom after the bell had rung. The door was propped open and Mia could see Safi talking to another boy by the patio door on the other side of the room. Safi pointed to the playground and Mia could hear him explaining the short cut to the hall. Safi turned round and saw her.

'I was just showing him the quick way to the hall,' said Safi, but the boy had already disappeared so they emptied their lockers and were soon stepping into the afternoon sunshine. The smell of newly cut grass filled the air. They began walking home. Mia's Nan was going to meet them half way.

The walk home always took a long time. There were several ponds that could only be accessed by narrow dirt tracks through straggly trees and hedges of bracken. They made a den and jumped across the stream and got wet feet pretending to escape from the Witch of Sardeeni through the horse's field. They were collecting logs to make a dam across the brook when they heard Bear barking and looked up to see Mia's Nan walking towards them. She had a kind face which broke into a ready smile when she saw them. She was quite tall, taller even than Safi's dad and had wild, curly white hair that bounced around her shoulders.

'What's for tea?' asked Safi as they were going down the back lane to the cottage.

'Well Mia tells me you like eggs, so omelette tonight.' Safi's face fell.

'She's joking,' Mia laughed. 'We've got pizza, haven't we Nan?'

'Yes with cans of cola and ice cream.' Safi's face lit up.

They dropped off their school bags and went to play in the back meadow with Bear. Mia's Nan watched them from the upstairs window. She was making some curtains and from her sewing table she could see them clearly.

The back field was higher than the surrounding land and Mia remembered that years ago it had been used for dumping household waste. Now it was a green meadow with clumps of nettles and blackberry thicket hedges. Curiously in the corner of the field there was a steep slope and Mia and Safi ran down it to the small copse of tangled willow trees at the bottom. The trees were twisted and just right for climbing. There was a dead tree trunk laying in the middle and they dared each other to run across it.

'Let's make this our special place,' said Safi. 'I like it here. We could collect stones and put them around the top of the slope. Look there are loads here.' So they began picking up the bigger stones and placing them around the rim of the slope so that they formed a circle and marked the place as their own. It was hard work. Mia was thirsty and was going to suggest they went back when Bear started barking.

'Look, even Bear's having fun,' said Safi. Bear was digging around some bricks and barking with excitement. 'What's he doing?' They went over to see what Bear was digging at.

'That's a badger's set,' Mia said. She felt quite proud of herself for knowing what a badger's set was. Safi looked puzzled. 'It's where a badger lives,' she explained, 'they dig really big holes and have tunnels under the ground.' Safi stiffened and looked down. 'Don't worry...' Mia continued, '...see these bricks in the hole. The farmer probably did that to make the badgers go away.'

'That's sad,' sighed Safi.

'Nan said badgers have diseases that cows can catch.'

'What's Bear after then?' Mia pushed Bear gently away and Safi brushed at the soil where Bear had been digging.

'Look there, what's that?' asked Mia seeing something in the ground. Safi pulled a small, round, flat object from the pile of dirt. It was about the size of a jammy dodger biscuit.

At that very moment a dark shadow fell over them. Mia felt as if someone had walked up behind her. She turned her head to look but no one was there, just a big cloud drifting in front of the setting sun.

'What's wrong?' Safi asked. Mia looked at him and shivered.

'Nothing,' she shrugged, 'just the sun playing tricks.' Bear leapt up the stony bank to the ridge and ran around the edge and the sun came out from behind the cloud and lit up the disc of wood in Safi's hand.

'What do you think it is?' asked Mia, prodding it with her finger.

'Don't know. Let's go back to your Nans and clean it off.' He added, 'I hope dinner's ready I'm starving.' They climbed up the slope and when they were at the top Mia looked across the field but there was no one there.

They cleaned off their find with warm, soapy water and an old toothbrush while they waited for their pizzas to cook, drying it off with kitchen roll. It was the size and thickness of a small biscuit and made of wood. Lines had been scored around the edge and roughly marked notches and grooves had been made with a knife on one side to form the image of a bird and on the other to scratch the letter T. Mia and Safi looked at it in wonder.

'What d'you think Nan?' asked Mia as her Nan put a plate of pizza slices in the middle of the table and gave them a plate each with instructions for them to wash their hands and tuck in.

'It looks like it's hand-made,' she said turning it over. 'What do you think?'

'That's definitely a T. I reckon that's the initial of the person who carved it,' said Safi taking a big bite of pizza.

'That's a good idea. Um… there's Tilly, Tamsin, Tammy, Trina…'

'Could be a boy though,' said Safi. 'What about Tom, there's a Tom in my class and a Toby.'

'Trevor?' offered Mia's Nan standing by the kitchen door holding a cup of tea.

'Or Tyson,' said Mia gulping back cola and supressing a burp. 'D'you think its Roman?'

'Or a Viking token from a game or something. We're doing the Vikings at school and they made wooden pieces for board games,' said Safi.

'I don't think it's that old,' said Mia's Nan, 'it would have rotted away in the ground if it was that old. It's probably less than a hundred years old. And what about the other side? Is that a bird do you think? A bird with a long cloak…look at that straight line there.' She pointed at the bird and traced her finger along the line.

They passed the wooden token between each other until

Mia's Nan took out her magnifying glass and handed it to Mia. Mia peered through the lens then suddenly drew in her breath in recognition.

'I know what it is. Look here.' She passed the magnifying glass to Safi so that he could see what she meant. 'Can you see? It's a magpie. Nan, look. It's a magpie.'

Mia left the wooden token on the mantel piece and after a few days other things began to take precedence. There was her weekly drama class with her friend Eloise and then she stayed with her grandad for a couple of days as most weekends her Nan worked a nightshift at the old people's home. It wasn't until Monday when she got back from school that she looked for the wooden disc with the magpie carved into it, but it was gone. She searched everywhere but couldn't find it.

Mia's Nan said she hadn't moved it and after taking everything off of the mantel piece she decided it must have fallen off. She checked Bear's bed and under all the furniture just in case it had rolled out of sight but she couldn't find it.

'I'll have another look while you're having your bath,' said Mia's Nan, 'it can't be far,' she smiled. 'When you're out of the bath we'll see if we can Skype mummy.' Mia felt a wave of excitement and forgot all about the strange wooden token.

In the bath she began thinking about all the things she wanted to tell her mum. The part she'd got in the school play, the after school dance class, the dens she'd made with Safi. It was hard not having her mum around for months at a time. She didn't know anyone else whose mum lived away. Grown-ups always said *Mia's so easy, she just gets on with it…*' but inside it didn't feel easy. No one really understood and Mia tried not to think about it too much. What was the point? She couldn't do anything about it.

Mia led in the rose smelling bubble bath with her eyes closed listening to the hypnotic drip of the tap. The water was cooling down quickly and her thoughts were beginning to drift. In her mind she went back to when she and Safi were in the field. There they were in her mind's eye playing on the old tree trunk. She could hear herself laughing and Safi suggesting they make a circle of stones. Then Bear barked and she watched her dream-self scrabble in the soil for the wooden token. But where was Safi? Was that him on the other side of the copse looking at her? Was that boy Safi? He was looking at her feet. Mia looked down too, to see what he was looking at. There was water bubbling up through the ground, it was freezing cold. It quickly reached her ankles. Suddenly a dark cloud cast a black shadow across her. The water was rising. It was like ice. It reached her knees.

Mia felt herself going under the water, struggling for breath but it wasn't a day dream any more. She thrashed around and managed to pull herself out of the bath spluttering, coughing and dragging air into her lungs with huge gulps. Suddenly back to reality she stood up shivering. She could feel her heart hammering in her chest. That's when she realized the sound of dripping water had stopped. She looked at the tap and there hung a slender icicle.

The bathroom door opened and as it did the icicle dropped into the bath.

'Mia you'll catch your death of cold. Come on lovely.' Mia's Nan took a fluffy towel from the cupboard and put it on the toilet seat. 'Out you come.' She didn't notice anything was wrong and went off to get the hair dryer.

Mia shivered. She bent down and reached into the water and retrieved a small sliver of ice. She held it in the palm of her hand and watched it quickly melt away. The tap began to drip again.

While Mia had been in the bath Mia's Nan had found the small disc of wood carved with the letter T.

'It was in the hollow bit at the back of the mantle-piece,' she said handing it to Mia. Brushing her damp hair Mia wondered what the T really stood for. Trouble she thought...

The next day Mia was quiet at school. She couldn't get the day dream she'd had in the bath out of her head. And what about the icicle? She was beginning to wonder if she'd imagined it. To make matters worse she hadn't even got to talk to her mum as the connection was down. Safi had asked her what was wrong but she just shrugged. She felt guilty about that. Maybe she should have told him. He was her friend after all.

That night she sat at the table in the back room trying to finish her homework but she was thinking about what had happened in the bath the night before. She held the wooden token she and Safi had found and traced the carving of the magpie with her finger.

Mia's Nan was in the garden having a cup of tea with Miss Jaggers who had brought a pile of old photographs of the village for Mia's Nan to go through. They were organising a history group open night in the church hall. Mia could hear their voices drifting in from the garden.

'Old Mr Bassett had a bad night on Sunday,' Mia's Nan was telling Miss Jaggers. 'Poor chap has nightmares. He kept ringing his buzzer. I didn't know whether I was coming or going. Thing is he was waking up some of the other old folk. I didn't even manage to sit down in my break.'

'Bassett? Bassett? That name rings a bell,' said Miss Jaggers. 'Is that Bobby Bassett?'

'That's the one, do you know him?'

'Well if it's who I'm thinking of I do. He used to live in the High Street a long time ago. His wife was lovely. A bit loud. Canadian!' she added as if that explained her loudness. 'Yes I remember now. Bobby Bassett was a village lad. I don't remember him very well I think he had a brother, but they were a lot older than me. His whole family upped sticks and immigrated to Canada when he was a teenager. He came back to the village about 20 years later with a wife and a couple of kids...' she sighed. 'Well I never...Bobby Bassett. Always had the weight of the world on his shoulders that boy.'

Mia had an idea. She stood up quickly and went into the garden.

'Hello young lady,' said Miss Jaggers as Mia came out into the evening sunshine.

'Are you stuck on your homework?' asked Mia's Nan. She took a sip from the mug of tea she cradled in her hand.

'No, I...um, sorry to interrupt but I was wondering if Miss Jaggers knows what this is?' She offered Miss Jagger the wooden disc to examine.

'Oo...what's this? Let me get my glasses on.' She rummaged in her large hand bag and produced a pair of snazzy red reading spectacles. She put them on and Mia gave her the token.

She examined it very carefully, turning it over several times. Mia explained what she thought the images were.

'...and where did you find it?' asked Miss Jaggers.

'Over in the field by the willow trees.'

'In the corner of the field?'

'Yeah, where the ground slopes down. Bear found it really, he was digging in an old badger hole.' Bear, who was half asleep on the grass gently thumped his tail on the ground at the mention of his name.

'Well, there is something familiar about it.' said Miss Jaggers rubbing her chin. 'Can I take a photo of it? I can ask my brother. He lives in Spain but we chat every week. He might be able to jog my memory.' She handed it back to Mia. '...and you say you found it by the willows on the field?'

'Yes. In the dip.'

'That's where we used to play as kids,' smiled Miss Jaggers as she unzipped a side pocket in her bag and took out her mobile. 'That's where the lake was we used to swim in, - though I suppose it was really a large pond. We called it the bather.' She found the camera app on her phone. 'Now Mia if you put the talisman on the table I'll take a few pictures of both sides and we'll decide which ones to send.'

24

'What's a talisman?' asked Mia as she placed it on the table.

'It's like a lucky charm,' said Mia's Nan.

'And the place we found it…it's where your bather lake was?' Mia asked. Miss Jaggers finished taking pictures of the token and nodded.

'Yes. It sounds like it from your description. We played there after the war, that's the Second World War I'm talking about Mia. Although the lake was filled in during the 1950's. That small slope with the bent willow trees where you found the talisman is all that's left.' Mia's gaze moved to the garden table. It was covered in photographs of men and women wearing clothes from older times and streets and buildings she thought she recognised.

'Are there any photos of our house or our lane here?' asked Mia.

'There are some photos of around this area Mia,' said her Nan, 'when Miss Jaggers and I have sorted them I'll put them aside for you to see. In the meantime haven't you got some homework to do?'

'I've done it. Well almost…can I ring Safi? Please Nan.' Mia did her best pleading expression. Her Nan tutted but nodded.

'Thanks for taking the pictures Miss Jaggers. I really hope your brother recognises it.' But before Miss Jaggers could answer Mia had run back into the house to call Safi.

Mia was relieved to tell Safi about the daydream she'd had in the bath where she was re-living the game that they'd played. How it had become frightening when water started bubbling out of the ground and she thought she was going to drown. She told him how she was somehow under the water in her real bath and how for a brief moment she struggled to get up and catch her breath. She told him about the dripping water turning into an icicle and how she held it in her hand until it melted.

Safi didn't laugh. Safi believed her. Mia was sorry she hadn't told him at school. She took a breath and went on to tell him about the wet swimsuit that had turned up in her bedroom…

'…and then there's the crying. I sometimes hear someone crying in the middle of the night.' Safi was quiet for a moment.

'Did anything like this happen before you and your Nan moved house?' he asked almost in a whisper.

'No…do you think it's something to do with the cottage?' asked Mia.

'I don't know…look try and get some sleep tonight and we can talk tomorrow. I might have some more ideas by then.' Mia was glad Safi was her friend. She knew he would try to help her find out what was happening.

'Ok…thanks for listening.'

'That's what friends are for,' he said. 'I will think about this tonight and maybe I will get some inspiration. And Mia…'

'Yes.'

'Have a shower next time.' Mia laughed. 'See you tomorrow.'

'See you tomorrow,' said Mia, 'and thanks for believing me.' She disconnected the call. It felt good to have told Safi what happened. She knew she could trust him and that he would try his best to help her. But although she felt relieved to have told someone, saying it out loud made it much more real. She shivered.

Mia's Nan and Miss Jaggers came indoors. It was getting cold outside, the sun had almost disappeared and a ribbon of red stretched across the horizon of an ever darkening sky.

'Do you want some hot chocolate Mia?' asked her Nan.

'Yes please.'

'Go and get your pyjamas on then and I'll fill the kettle.' Miss Jaggers and Mia's Nan were bringing in the old photographs and Mia could see that the ones Miss Jaggers held were beginning to slip from her grasp. Within seconds photos were falling to the floor and Mia rushed to catch them. Mia's Nan and Miss Jaggers put their photos on the table and Mia knelt on the floor picking up the ones that had slid under the chair. 'There's one more, just over there,' said Mia's Nan pointing at an old curling photograph that was caught under the skirting board. Mia picked it up and looked at it.

It was a black and white picture of a group of boys. They were wearing shirts and all but one of them had short trousers. The ones with short trousers had long grey socks and heavy boots. A couple of them wore sleeveless stripy jumpers over their shirts and one of them had a heavy jacket that was a bit tight. They all had short hair with neat partings. Mia looked closer.

'Look Nan…there's our house.' Mia's Nan peeped over Mia's shoulder and a look of recognition spread across her face. The boys were all stood in the field behind the row of cottages. They had their backs to the cottages and the camera captured not only the boys but the little dwellings behind them.

'Do you know anything about these boys or this photo Mary?' asked Mia's Nan. Miss Jaggers took the photo from Mia and looked at it really carefully.

'Well I never,' she exclaimed. 'That's my brother Bernard. Mrs Marshall gave me these photos for the history group when her husband died and I just put them in the history group box.' She looked at Mia. 'Bernard's the one with the jacket on. He loved that jacket, even when it was too small for him he squeezed into it. And that one there with one sock down his leg that's Dennis Gregory. He was a looker, he'd come round our house to call for Bernard and my heart would beat so fast...' She broke into laughter like barking.

'Oh Meg, look – there's Bobby Bassett...the old chap that kept you up all night at the old folks home.' She hesitated – 'Or is this one Bobby? I remember now, he was one of twins. He had a twin brother so I don't know which is which.' Mia's Nan squinted trying to see if either boy resembled the old man she looked after.

Mia looked closely and noticed something strange. All the boys were holding something up in front of them to show to the camera. A small object held between their fingers like a large coin or a round cracker or...

'The token, look Nan, their all holding something that looks like the token we found.' Mia picked up the wooden disc and held it up in the same way as the boys in the picture.

'It certainly looks the same shape and size Mia. But we'll never know for sure because the picture's too small. We can't really see exactly what they're holding.'

'It's the talisman. I know it is.' Mia was trying to work something out in her head. 'They've all got one. That means the one we found isn't the only one. Just think one of these boys is holding this actual one. But who? Who did this one belong to?' Mia's Nan was deep in thought.

'There are seven boys. Seven...' She repeated.

'Seven for a secret never to be told,' whispered Mia to herself.

Mia brushed her hair then got into bed and read to her Nan for a while. She was reading the story of the boy who cried wolf. It was part of the homework she'd been struggling with earlier. She had to choose an old story with a moral. A story that shows how you should or shouldn't behave and then make up a modern story with the same idea.

The boy who cried wolf was a shepherd who was bored with minding the sheep and kept crying 'wolf, wolf!' The villagers would come running thinking a wolf was attacking the sheep but all along it was just the shepherd boy pretending. Eventually he cried 'wolf' when there was a real wolf and nobody came. It was a story that explained that if you tell lies then when you eventually tell the truth, no one believes you.

'I don't like the shepherd boy,' said Mia.

'No, he wasn't very nice was he?'

'Did the wolf eat him?' asked Mia, 'It doesn't say in the story.'

'I hope not,' said Mia's Nan. 'He probably learnt his lesson after that!'

'It's hard thinking of a modern story,' said Mia.

'Hm…what about when we used to play at the park and you'd come running to me to say you'd found a puppy in a bush. I'd dash over full of anticipation and find out it was a 'pretend' puppy. Then one day you said 'Nan, I've found a puppy' and I told you to stop making up stories, but you dragged me to the ditch behind the swings and there really was a puppy.'

'Bear…' smiled Mia. 'That's a good story. I'll use that one because it has a happy ending.'

'Time for lights out now,' said Mia's Nan kissing her and tucking her in, 'night sweetheart.'

'Night Nan, see ya in the morning.'

*   *   *

Mia was dreaming and in her dream she heard a voice shouting '*help me, help me*'. It was a boy's voice. Over and over again he was calling for help. In her dream Mia was in the field behind her Nan's cottage. She was walking away from the willow trees in the hollow. Walking away from the place where Bear had dug up the talisman. Walking away from the spot where Miss Jaggers had swum in the bather as a little girl. Walking away from the boy shouting '*help me, help me*'. It was cold. Snow was gently falling and settling on the ground. She was with a group of children. Boys. She put her hand in her pocket and could feel a round, wooden disc. '*Help me!*' shouted the boy's voice and she woke up.

Mia opened her eyes and knew she was in her bedroom, she could vaguely see the outline of her chest of drawers. There was a shaft of light cast by the moon across her duvet where the curtains weren't pulled quite together. She sighed and her eyelids began to feel heavy again. Just as she began to relax she heard it. Immediately she was wide awake. She lay very still and listened. There it was again. It wasn't her imagination. There was definitely someone crying.

She lay motionless, heeding every sound, trying to work out where the sobbing was coming from. Outside. Yes, it was definitely outside, but close, very close. She was too frightened to get up and look out of her window and just lay there for what seemed hours, listening to the heart breaking sound of what she was sure now was a child crying. At some point she must have fallen asleep because when she eventually woke up her Nan was in her room taking her school clothes out of the cupboard.

'Morning Mia, I'm just going to walk Bear in the field out the back for 10 minutes. You'll be able to see me from the window. While I'm gone get yourself dressed and I'll warm up your pain au chocolat when I get in.' She led Mia's school clothes on the bottom of the bed and opened the curtains. The morning light flooded her room. 'Mia, are you awake?'

She bent over and kissed her cheek. 'Come on lovely…I'll be back in 10 minutes, move yourself.'

Mia grunted and stretched, then everything that had happened in the night came flooding back to her. She was surprized that she felt more curious than scared. What was happening? Was it her imagination? She got dressed, brushed her hair and walked over to the window. There was an old hornbeam tree at the end of the garden and she watched a magpie hop into the twisted branches with a twig in its mouth. Her Nan and Bear were walking back to the cottage. She waved but her Nan didn't see her.

Mia picked up her school bag and went downstairs. She took a packet of crisps from the larder for Safi and diluted some blackcurrant squash to drink. Walking into the back room she saw the pile of photographs. The picture of the boys holding their wooden talismans was on the top. She picked it up and looked closely at all the faces.

There was Miss Jaggers' brother with his tightly fitted jacket, taller than the others with an air of arrogance about him. Then Dennis Gregory, he sported a neat parting in his wavy black hair. He must have moved when the photograph was taken as his face was slightly blurred. …And there was Bobby Bassett. Or was it his twin brother? Two boys were identical, how they looked was the same and what they wore was the same, but Mia could see they were different from their expressions. One held his head high and had a cheeky grin on his face the other looked more serious with his head down and his eyes lifted to catch the camera. She put the photograph in her bag with the crisps. Safi would have a lot to think about when she saw him later.

Mia was looking forward to meeting Safi to see if he'd come up with any ideas about the icicle in her bath, her wet swimsuit or the crying she heard in the night. She was sat at her desk in class. There were 20 minutes to go before the dinner bell and everyone was reading quietly while Miss Shelley marked homework and checked everyone's reading record. Mia liked Miss Shelley. She was firm but fair. She didn't tolerate messing around or shouting out but was always willing to give everyone a chance. She had brown hair that fell around her pale face and delicate hands with nicely rounded nails that Mia always admired.

Mia was staring at the page of her book but her thoughts were far away. She began to think about the photograph of the boys. Mia had gotten Miss Jaggers to take a picture of it and send it to her brother in Spain with the pictures she'd taken of the talisman. Mia wondered if anyone else in the old photo was still alive. There was Miss Jaggers' brother, Dennis Gregory and the twins, but who were the other three boys? They'd all be really old now she thought. She really hoped Miss Jaggers' brother would remember them, would remember anything.

Mia sighed. She really wanted to talk to her mum about it all but Monday had been her last chance to speak to her before her mum went on manoeuvres for four weeks. They'd had a quick conversation on the phone at the weekend but Mia hadn't said anything about the weird things that had been happening. She didn't want her mum to worry. What she wanted more than anything was for her mum to hold her tight and tell her how much she loved her and that everything would be alright.

Her desk was next to the window and the warmth of the sun was intensified by the glass, making her feel muggy headed and sleepy. She could hear someone talking to Miss Shelley, but their voice sounded like a distant murmur, like a bee buzzing around a flower. The words on the page of her book looked blurry. Her eyelids began to feel heavy and she felt her head start to fall.

'Bang!' she jolted upright not quite sure what had happened. Everyone was looking at her, no, not at her but at the window next to her.

'What on earth was that?' Miss Shelley asked as she stood up and rushed to the window.

'It was a bird Miss,' a voice blurted from the back of the class. 'I saw it, it flew right into the window.' Miss Shelley walked up to Mia's desk and looked out of the window, quickly followed by half the children in the class straining to see if there really was a bird. Mia could see clearly as she was sat the closest.

There on the ground outside there was a bird. A big bird and it wasn't moving. Mia watched holding her breath, she thought it was dead.

'Oh dear,' Miss Shelley said. 'Sometimes on bright days the reflection of the sky or trees in the window can make a bird think it's flying through the air and it ends up flying straight into a window.'

'Is it dead?' someone piped up. 'Shall I get the caretaker?' Miss Shelley hesitated. She turned to Mia.

'Did that give you a fright Mia?'

'A bit...' said Mia. It had certainly woken her up. She looked out of the window. 'Look Miss, look, it's still alive.' Mia felt a great sense of relief. The bird quickly got up and flapped its feathers as if they were sticky. Shiny, black-blue feathers, laced with white. Mia was so glad it was alive. It hopped into the bush.

'It's just stunned. Imagine running into a brick wall,' said Miss Shelley. 'I think it'll be fine.'

Mia knew there was something more happening than just a bird mistaking a reflection in a window for the clear, blue sky. Was someone trying to tell her something and if so, what was it?

'It would have smashed straight into your face if the

window hadn't been there,' said Jake.

'Yes,' answered Mia. 'I think I've got the message anyway.' Jake didn't really know what she meant by that, but Mia knew. The bird that had smashed into the window was a magpie. One for sorrow thought Mia.

12

Safi and Mia walked to the end of the school field after they'd eaten lunch. They were trying to hide from Jake who wanted to play Warriors of Albion.

'So, what happened in your class before dinner?' asked Safi excitedly as they walked. 'Suicidal birds I hear.'

'Magpie. It was a magpie,' corrected Mia. Safi looked thoughtful as they sat down beneath an old oak tree and leant against the rough bark of its broad trunk.

'Magpies popping up again?' Safi said almost to himself. 'Magpie on the token too.'

'Yes…is it just a coincidence do you think?'

'I don't know,' said Safi, 'what are the other common themes?'

'What do you mean?'

'Well what else comes up again and again?'

'Water…water. My swimming costume, the ice in my bath, my dream about the water coming through the ground.'

'So we have magpies and water…'

'And someone crying,' said Mia. 'And this too…' she said eagerly pulling the photograph out of her bag.

'This is an old picture taken behind my house just after the Second World War. Look at what they're holding.' She thrust the grainy photograph in front of Safi's face. 'You can see what they're holding too, can't you? I know I'm right.' Safi's face took on a creamy pallor and his dark eyes widened. The picture began to shake and Mia realised that it wasn't the picture but Safi's hand that was shaking. 'Saf are you alright?' she asked. 'Safi…' Safi was staring at the picture, his face frozen, half fear and half disbelief. 'Saf, Saf, you're frightening me.'

Mia pulled the photograph out of his hand and he began to breathe really oddly in deep, deep breaths. He was dragging the air into his lungs in huge, long gulps, sucking in the oxygen, but it didn't seem to have any affect. His lips were turning blue, his eyes were beginning to bulge.

'I'm getting help…Safi, Safi,' Mia cried. 'I'm getting help.' Safi gripped Mia's hand as if to say 'don't leave me' but Mia knew that she would have to get someone. Tears were in her eyes, she would have to get someone immediately. 'I'll come straight back. I promise.'

She didn't want to leave him but she tore her hand away from his and ran. She ran faster than she'd ever run before and all the time she was shouting, screaming for help. The sun blazed down and she could feel sweat running down her back, her long hair stuck to her face like wet ribbon but she kept on running knowing deep down that Safi's life depended on it.

'Help,' she screamed as she ran onto the playground. Miss Shelley was running towards her, she was a blur, everything was blurred. 'Safi, its Safi' she cried. 'He's at the end of the field…he can't breathe. Help him…help him…please, help him…'

Everything happened at once, Miss Shelley blew a whistle and all the children stopped in their tracks. She was saying something to two of the dinner ladies and Mr Forrest ran over. As Miss Shelley and Mr Forrest ran back across the playing field to find Safi one of the dinner ladies tapped out a number on a mobile phone and the other put her arm around Mia.

'Don't worry lovely, it'll all be ok.' Mia tasted the salty tears that ran down her cheeks and her throat was sore with sobbing. Someone took her into the little room by the office and the receptionist held her hand and told her that she'd been very brave and gave her orange squash. Mia didn't feel brave. Mia felt sad, very, very sad and very confused.

Before long she heard the siren of an ambulance and all she could think of was Safi. 'Is Safi alright?' she asked the receptionist but her only reply was that he was being looked after. Mia wanted to scream. She buried her head in her hands.

Miss Shelley came in then and put her arm around Mia.

'Well done Mia, because of you Safi's got the help he needed really quickly. That must have been so scary.'

'I…It was more scary for Saf.' Saying his name brought more tears. 'I…I couldn't do anything…I didn't want to leave him. Really I didn't. But I had to. I had to.' Mia blurted.

'I know. But you did the right thing. I've called your Nan, she'll be here in a minute.' Miss Shelley stayed there with her arm around Mia until her Nan arrived.

When Mia saw her Nan she threw her arms around her neck and held her as tightly as she could. Her Nan rocked her gently and whispered softly.

'I've just spoken to Safi's mum Mia, he's stable. He's going to be alright and later on tonight when he's recovered a little bit you're allowed to see him. Just for a little while because he still needs a lot of rest.' Mia pressed her face into her Nan's shoulder, tears running down her cheeks. She breathed in the floral scent of fabric softener mixed with the earthy smell of Bear and felt a little bit better. Deep down though, she knew nothing would be right again until she'd seen Safi.

13

Mia's Nan drove them home then tucked Mia up in a fleecy, red blanket on the sofa in the living room. Mia held her Nan's hand and began to drift into a calming sleep. She could hear birds singing outside and her face felt warm from the sun shining through the window. She fell into a sleep that was dreamless, a place of silent blackness that was warm and comforting.

When she woke up she could hear her Nan talking in the kitchen. She lay there for a while with her eyes closed remembering everything that had happened, reliving it. She wiped away a tear and took a deep breath remembering what her Nan had said about Safi being alright. She desperately wanted to see him and stood up and wandered through to the kitchen.

'Well here's my little heroine,' said her Nan putting her arm around her. 'Did you get some sleep?' Mia nodded and smiled weakly.

'Who were you talking to?' she asked.

'Mary, Mary Jaggers, we were chatting on the phone. She sends her love and hopes you're feeling better.' Mia's Nan reached for the kettle and filled it with water at the sink. 'Let's have a cuppa and then I'll ring Safi's mum and see what time we can go and see him.'

'What time is it now?' asked Mia feeling a bit confused.

'Just gone five, you've been asleep around three hours.'

'Did Miss Jaggers say anything about writing to her brother?' asked Mia sitting on the stool in the corner of the kitchen while her Nan took out some cups and saucers.

'Yes, she said she's sent him the pictures and asked him about the boys and the token. He hasn't written back yet but I'm sure he will.' Mia's Nan took out some milk and sugar. 'Do you want sugar in your tea?' She looked at Mia and winked. Mia couldn't help smiling as she wasn't normally allowed sugar.

'Yes, two please.' Mia's Nan made the tea and they sipped the warm liquid and dunked chocolate chip cookies. Then Mia's Nan called Safi's mum who gave them the go ahead to visit him in hospital.

∗   ∗   ∗

At the hospital Mia's Nan and Safi's mum were talking quietly by the window of Safi's room. Mia stood by Safi's bed. He was sleeping. Plastic tubes were attached to his nostrils feeding him oxygen and his hand was bruised where sticking plaster held a device in place that allowed the nurse to give him injections. Mia felt numb and her throat was dry. She swallowed then quickly looked over her shoulder to make sure no one was listening. She leaned in towards Safi and whispered his name. Nothing. She tried again but a little louder.

'Saf, Safi.' He blinked a few times and opened his eyes. He smiled. Mia knew immediately he was alright. She sighed with relief and smiled back. 'Oh Saf, I was so worried. What happened at school? What happened to you?'

'It's called an asthma attack,' said a voice behind them. It was Safi's mum. She looked kindly at Mia with her big, dark eyes. Her hair was hidden by a black scarf. She wore a flowery top and a pair of jeans. Her English was stilted with a heavy accent, but she spoke slowly and Mia understood every word she said. 'It's happened before, a long time ago when Safi was very young. When we were in Iraq. There was a...' her voice became shaky and hesitant. 'There was a...an explosion. It was in the um...market... close to our house. I was buying a water melon. We were near...we were near the blast but by some miracle were not injured. But Safi...Safi had a bad asthma attack. He was very young and they said it was because of the bomb exploding. They said it triggered his attack.' She looked sad. 'There were often explosions. The noise, the fear...the fear...it would always cause an asthma attack. Since we have come to England Safi has not had any problems…never…until now.'

'What caused it?' asked Mia, 'there were no explosions, there was nothing that would have…' she was going to say 'frightened Safi', but she stopped, suddenly remembering the photograph that he was looking at when he had the asthma attack.

'The doctor thinks that maybe some pollen from a flower or tree has caused it…we don't really know.'

'But they can do something about it can't they?' asked Mia.

'Yes. Safi can take medicine. He will have to carry an inhaler in case this thing happens again, but…' and she smiled, 'he will be alright.'

'Can Mia stay for a while?' asked Safi. He was pushing himself up on his elbows. Mia's Nan suggested that she and Safi's mum get themselves a drink from a coffee machine she had seen down the corridor and they left the room leaving Mia and Safi alone.

'What happened at school?' she asked again. 'What happened?'

'The photograph. The photograph of the boys.' His eyes grew large.

'What about it?'

'There are two boys in the photograph that look the same. Twins I suppose,' he spoke quietly.

'Yes, I was going to tell you about them. Miss Jaggers told me their surname was Bassett. One of them is called Bobby, Bobby Bassett. And you know what? He's still alive. He lives at the old people's home where Nan works.' Safi listened carefully to everything Mia said.

'You know the day I came to your house and you waited for me outside my class?' Mia nodded. 'Do you remember I was showing a boy the short cut to the hall from the patio door of my classroom?'

'Yes. I remember.' Safi looked dazed.

'The boy that I gave directions to…' his voice faltered momentarily but he was deadly serious. 'He…he's the same boy as in the picture. Mia…He's one of those twin boys.' A

45

shiver ran down Mia's spine and her knees felt like jelly. All sorts of things were racing through her head.

'Are you sure?' She tried to smile. 'You boys all look the same,' she joked. 'And anyway, it's a really old picture…it's easy to make mistakes especially after what happened. The asthma attack, it was terrible, you can't be thinking straight.'

'Mia…I had the attack because I recognised him…Even his clothes were the same…at the time I didn't really think about it. Classes are always dressing up as Romans or Victorians…' His voice tailed off and he stared at Mia. 'I think you should stop trying to find out about the token and the crying you hear in the night. Try to forget it…leave it alone.'

'I can't Saf. And now you've told me this it's more important than ever that I find out what's happening.'

'If you carry on you could be in danger Mia. Leave it alone.' He grabbed her arm and squeezed it tightly. His expression was grim as he stared into her eyes and repeated 'Leave it alone.'

'I can't.'

'Remember what happened in the bath. You could have drowned. I could have died. It's too dangerous. Leave it alone.'

Just then the door opened and Safi's mum walked in.

'Time's up now. More rest for you Safi and hopefully home tomorrow.' Mia's Nan stood at the door.

'We'll visit Safi again soon Mia. Fingers crossed he'll be at home, but time to go now.' Mia looked at Safi. She could see the concern on his face. She sighed.

'I'll see you tomorrow Saf.' He smiled weakly.

'We can catch up on Warriors of Albion – there's a competition on CBBC to visit the set and meet the cast. We can enter that,' he said. Mia nodded. Her Nan held the door open for her and ushered her out.

Mia leant her head against the window of the car as her Nan drove them home. She watched the countryside go by as the light of day began to fade and felt a well of determination rise up inside of her. She had to get to the bottom of what was happening. She was not going to give up. She was going to unravel the puzzle of the boy and the crying, the magpie token and the icy water. She was going to find out what was going on if it was the last thing she did!

14

Several days passed and it was almost as if nothing had happened. Safi was back at school and Mia had not been woken by someone crying in the night. That morning Mia's Nan woke her up for school as usual. Bear had followed her upstairs and had jumped on Mia's bed.

'I've got to go to the old people's home straight from dropping you off at school to cover for someone who's on holiday,' she said, 'so I'm just taking Bear over the back field for ten minutes to give him a quick run around. Please be up and dressed by the time I get back. No dillydallying!' She put Mia's brush on the dressing table, '...and maybe even brush your hair...'

'Ugh...' grunted Mia.

'Ten minutes. Be up. Please.' Her Nan left the room and ushered Bear down the stairs.

Mia turned onto her back and stretched, then yawned. She could hear the radio blasting out downstairs. She opened her eyes and looked over at her school clothes hanging on the back of her chair. Sitting up she stretched again and pulled back the duvet. Mia walked sleepily to her dressing table, picked up her reading book and put it in her school bag. As she brushed her hair she looked out of the window.

The weather had become hot which meant every morning a mist hung over the back field until the heat of the sun cut through it to reveal dewy, green grass and sparkling spider's webs. Today was no exception. Mia could see her Nan and Bear walking up the track in the middle of the field away from the cottages, the hazy white mist was still thick so they looked distant and out of focus. Mia looked closer. There was something else. Someone else. Who was that with her Nan?

There was another figure. Someone shorter. Maybe a child. Maybe a boy. As she watched, this person placed a hand on Bear's back and Bear ran away into the mist. Mia watched as her Nan and this other person also disappeared into the mist.

Mia screwed up her eyes trying to see through the white haze but there was no one there. She felt her heart begin to race. 'Nan...Nan...' she spoke aloud, pressing her face against the window. Then suddenly she was tearing off her night clothes and pulling her polo shirt over her head. She half hopped into her skirt as she left her room and leapt down the stairs just avoiding a collision with the dining table. She didn't stop to put on her shoes but raced out of the back door bare footed. She sprinted up the garden path and unlatched the back gate, pulling it open with a grunt.

'Hello love.' Her Nan was stood at the gate with Bear panting at her side. 'I'm very impressed I didn't think you'd get up *this* quickly.' She glanced down at Mia's feet. 'Socks and shoes might be an idea though.' Mia was confused.

'I couldn't see you...' she said.

'I know. It's so misty out there. You can't see your hand in front of your face.' Mia's Nan closed the gate and they walked back towards the house. 'Breakfast then, pain au chocolat?' Mia wasn't listening.

'I couldn't see you...Bear, he went running off and then you disappeared.'

'Yes, I think he smelt a rabbit or maybe that fox that lives by the willows.' They were indoors now and Mia's Nan was getting breakfast ready. Mia took a breath.

'Was there anyone else out there?' Mia's Nan stopped what she was doing and looked at Mia.

'What do you mean?'

'Well just before Bear ran off I thought I saw someone else. Someone with you and Bear,' she hesitated. 'A child. A boy maybe.' Mia's Nan began to fill the kettle.

'No one else there Mia. Just me and Bear. The mist can play tricks on you though. Not just on your eyes. It can pick up sounds and move them around. I could have sworn I heard people talking in the mist. Mumbling.'

'Weren't you scared?' asked Mia.

'It was just mumbling, probably a combination of birds,

the stream and cars on the main road all being shaken up and redistributed in the mist. It's all explainable by science – I'm just not a scientist. Now, get some socks and shoes on and come and have breakfast.'

15

'You're still trying to find out about the crying boy aren't you?' said Safi as they sat in the shade of the pagoda in the school garden at lunch time.

'How do you know it's a boy?' asked Mia.

'It just seems more likely…the boy that spoke to me in school, the photo, the dream you had…' Mia pressed her lips together, she didn't want to say anything that would upset Safi in case he had another asthma attack. There was a quiet moment then Safi said. 'I've had an idea.' Mia didn't reply, she looked at him curiously. 'The day I saw the boy in the photograph he asked me how to get to the hall. Well, there's been a school here since Victorian times but my classroom with the patio doors to the playground wouldn't have been built back then. It probably didn't exist at the time the boys in the photo went to school either.' Mia was puzzled. 'Don't you see? He didn't know the way to the hall. If he was a village boy he probably came to school here…but back then my classroom didn't exist.'

'So…'

'Ask yourself Mia – why did he want to go to the hall?' Mia shrugged. 'Think about it. What's in the hall?'

'Um…nothing. It's a hall.'

'What's on the wall?' Mia suddenly realised what Safi was talking about.

'Photographs. Old photographs of kids that came to the school.'

'Exactly, what if the boy is trying to tell us where to look for clues. And what if one of those photographs holds a clue?'

'But where are the clues leading?' asked Mia. Safi shrugged.

'Maybe we'll find out who the crying boy is and why he's crying.' Safi got up. Mia was reluctant to move.

'But…you said, 'Leave it alone' – you said it was

dangerous. And what about you? I couldn't bare it if...'

'Mia. You're not going to leave it alone are you? And me? Well I know I'd feel happier knowing what's going on.'

'Ok then...' Mia stood up. 'You don't know how much better I feel knowing you're helping me Saf. Let's go look in the hall.'

*   *   *

The last dinner sitting was almost finished and nobody took any notice of Mia and Safi. The photographs were displayed on the back wall. They were sepia coloured and mounted on cream card with plain, dark wood frames. The date and names of the children in the photograph were printed on a card below.

There were about 15 pictures and the dates were random. 'When was the Second World War?' asked Mia. 'I'm sure Miss Jaggers said that's when they used to play on the field. When the brick works had been abandoned.'

'That's the 1940's I think,' said Safi.

There were only three photos for the 1940's and none showed the boys from the history group's photograph.

'Look.' Mia pointed at a photograph dated 1950. There were 7 boys and 5 girls in the photograph. None of them wore a school uniform and they were aged between about 10 and 13. 'Here's the boys. All of them. How come they're in the same class?' She was puzzled.

'It was only a small village,' said Safi. 'Probably had to put different age groups together.' He was looking at the words printed below the photographs. 'Here's all their names...' He began reading the boy's names out loud. '...Bernard Jaggers, Dennis Gregory, Paul Marshall, Colin Keyes, Gerald Manders, Bobby Bassett and Tommy Bassett.' He sighed - 'I think we just discovered the owner of our wooden token Mia. It's him.' He pointed at the sullen looking boy in the picture. 'Or him...' he pointed at the twin.

'Tommy Bassett,' she sighed. 'The letter T cut into the

54

back of the token. It's for Tommy. It's almost like he wanted us to know who he was. He came to *you* asking where the hall was didn't he Saf? Why would he do that unless he wanted to give us a clue, a clue to find out who he was? I think it's about time I asked Nan if I could visit Bobby Bassett in the old people's home. I think it's time to find out the truth about the crying boy.'

16

It was nearly midsummer. The days were long and the nights were short. Mia liked to leave her curtains open when she went to bed so that when she woke up in the morning her room was filled with light. But today it wasn't the rising sun that woke her, it was something else that startled Mia into wakefulness. She heard a sound and opened her eyes and caught sight of something spinning on her bedroom floorboards. She lifted her head to see more clearly. In the dawn light it looked like a wooden disc, the magpie talisman. Eventually it lost momentum, wobbled and fell flat. She sat up trying to make sense of what she'd seen.

Her eyes drifted to her table, the magpie token that she and Safi had found was exactly where she'd left it the night before. If the token was on her table what was that on the floor? As she sat up she noticed other tokens on her bedroom floor. She counted them. One, two, three and the one she'd seen spinning made four.

Mia moved to the edge of her bed and stared at the four tokens on the floor. Everything was silent. Mia was confused. The air in her room bristled momentarily as if energized by an electrical current and then gave way to a cool morning chill. Mia felt her heart pounding. She wanted to call her Nan, she opened her mouth but no words came out.

The birds singing outside brought Mia to her senses. She pulled back the covers and stepped out of bed. Kneeling down she gazed at each of the discs. They were roughly the same size and shape as the one she and Safi had found by the willows. On the side facing up, each was carved with a picture of a bird, a magpie. They were all similar but not quite the same, as if each were made by a different person. 'By a different boy…' Mia whispered out loud. She slowly turned over one of the tokens. Her hand was shaking. On the other side was the initial 'D'. She lay it back on the floor with the letter side up. 'Dennis Gregory', she said. Then she turned over the other tokens one by one.

As she turned each one over she said the name of the boy whose initial was displayed. 'Paul Marshall, Colin Keyes, Gerald Manders'. She stretched up to her table and took the original token and placed it on her bedroom floor with the others. '...Tommy Bassett.' Mia stared at the tokens. What did they mean? Where had they come from and why her?

Suddenly the whole room was filled with a flash of light and an explosive clap of thunder shook the house. Mia was startled and looked up, a few gentle spots of rain tapped against her window. Then out of nowhere the heaviest of downpours fell from the sky. The rain turned to hail and large marbles of ice hammered against the glass. Mia thought it would break her window. She stood up and looked out across the field. In the distance she could just make out a figure walking away from the cottages. She held her breath. It stopped and stood still for a moment as if whoever it was knew Mia was watching. And then slowly, very slowly it turned around.

Mia pressed her face against the window but the heavy rain made it difficult to see and she wondered if it was just her imagination. There was so much that she didn't understand. She picked up one of the five magpie tokens. It was as real as her hairbrush. She tried to understand where they could have come from. Was it magic? Was it a ghost? She put the tokens in her old pencil case and put it into her back pack. She had to show Safi.

17

At lunchtime the next day Safi and Mia sat under the pagoda. Safi examined the magpie talismans turning them over and over, hoping the answers would pop into his head. He said he'd read a ghost story where a teapot had appeared out of nowhere and poured a cup of tea but it was only a story.

'We need to speak to Bobby Bassett,' said Safi, but the question was, would he speak to them?

'It's the history group at Nan's tonight. Miss Jaggers might have heard from her brother.' Safi made her promise to ring him if she found anything out. Mia nodded. 'I'll ask Nan if you can come back after school tomorrow. We're in it together now Saf.'

The rest of the day dragged but at last the bell rang and Mia raced out of school. Mia's Nan and Bear were waiting at the back gate but Mia could see immediately that her Nan didn't look her usual smiley self.

'What's wrong Nan?' she asked.

'I've locked myself out.'

'What do you mean?' asked Mia.

'Well I locked the back door when I walked Bear this afternoon and when I went back for a quick cuppa before I picked you up the key wasn't where I'd left it.'

'Where did you leave it?'

'Behind the stone fairy in the garden. The door's still locked. I looked through the window everything looks ok, I just can't work out what's happened to the key.'

'Are you sure you left it behind the stone fairy?'

'Absolutely one hundred percent.'

'Let's go back and have another look,' suggested Mia. They walked home despondently, taking a short cut through the back field. It was overcast and a feisty breeze pulled at the long grass. Bear chased a rabbit and a sky lark hovered, singing a throaty melody.

As they opened the back gate they could hear the loud

'chakka chakka' call of magpies in the garden. Mia went straight to the stone fairy and searched for the key. She moved all the herb tubs and the pots of lavender and pansies.

'Are you sure you didn't hide it *under* something?' asked Mia.

'I'm sure,' said her Nan. The magpies began their screechy chattering again. Mia looked at the hornbeam tree and remembered something.

'Nan, can you get the ladder out of the shed?' Mia's Nan gave her a puzzled look. 'Please…'

'What for?'

'I just want to check something,' said Mia. Her Nan pulled the old wooden ladder out of the shed and Mia asked her to put it up against the hornbeam tree.

'If this is some silly prank Mia Page I'll…' Mia interrupted. 'No Nan, honest…let me just see…'

With the ladder in place Mia began to climb. She could hear the chakering screech of the magpies in the tree and as she got higher they flew raggedly out of the hornbeam sending a few leaves and a feather down onto her head. She moved slightly and the ladder wobbled.

'Nan, are you holding on to the bottom?' Mia called. All she could see were the leafy branches around her.

'Yes Mia. I'm holding it tight.'

Mia looked up, she could see the Magpie's nest. Just two more rungs to go. She stepped up to the next rung one foot at a time and then moved her hands up a rung as well. Then she repeated the action but this time she became confused. She'd stepped up with one foot but couldn't find the rung with her other foot. Her palms were sweaty and began to slip. She panicked, desperately trying to find the ladder rung with her toes but there was nothing there.

Suddenly she felt something hold onto her foot. She froze. She thought that she might be pulled from the ladder and fall to the ground. It was as if an invisible hand dragged at her foot. Just as she was about to cry out she felt the solid rung of the ladder beneath her toes. She looked down almost sure she would see that her Nan had come to her rescue, - but no one was there.

Mia took a breath. She told herself it was her imagination but deep down she knew something else had happened, she just didn't know what. Was something trying to help her or harm her? Was Safi right all along? Was her stubborn persistence in trying to find out what was happening at Magpie Cottage leading her into danger? She honestly didn't know.

'What are you doing?' called Mia's Nan. Mia shuffled slightly and leant over a thick bough so that she could look down on the magpie's nest. She let out a gasp. There in the nest were six greenish, brown eggs and nestled into the twigs was the back door key. There was something else too.

'Hang on,' Mia called reaching carefully into the nest making sure she didn't touch the eggs. She retrieved the items she'd discovered. She put them in her skirt pocket and began to climb down.

At the bottom Mia showed her Nan what she had found. As well as the key there was a pretty little golden ring with a sparkling emerald set in tiny diamonds. Mia's Nan was overjoyed.

'I lost that ring months ago digging up bricks in the garden! Your uncle gave it to me when you were born.' Mia could see tears of happiness in her Nan's eyes. With a look of elation she put it on her finger. 'What on earth gave you that mad idea?'

'I saw a magpie going into the tree with a twig in its beak a few weeks ago,' said Mia '…and I've read stories about magpies stealing things.'

'Let's get the kettle on Mia.' She held the little key aloft. 'Well done my lovely, you've saved the day.' Mia's Nan wrapped her arm around Mia's shoulder and kissed her head.

18

After they'd raided the cake tin Mia's Nan decided to hide a spare key in the shed just in case the back door key went missing again. Mia started downloading and printing animal pictures for a school project and Bear did what Bear did best, - ate his tea and fell asleep on the settee.

After a Chinese Chow Mein pot noodle and a large bowl of salt and vinegar crisps Mia began doing the jobs she would normally do on history group night. She put the cups on the tray and laid some shortbread biscuits on the willow patterned plate. She was just searching for the custard creams when there was a knock on the door.

'You're early Mary.' She heard her Nan say.

'Ah…I wanted to see Mia.' Miss Jaggers walked through to the back room. She held up an email she'd printed out and exclaimed.

'They're all dead, my dear! This is an email from my brother Bernard in Spain. He says all the boys in your photograph are dead but for him and poor old Bobby Bassett.' Mia's Nan went to put the kettle on while Miss Jaggers seated herself on an old wicker chair. Her brother had sent her a list of the boy's names and this corresponded with the names that Safi and Mia had got from the photograph at school.

Mia's mind was alive with thoughts. Upstairs in a pencil case in her back pack were five magpie tokens. She didn't even begin to understand how they'd come into her possession. The initials on the tokens were the initials of the dead boys in the photo. She knew for sure that someone was trying to tell her something, whether for good or ill, she just had to work out what they were trying to say and what she was meant to do.

'And the token? What about that? Did your brother recognise it?'

'Indeed he did. He has one too apparently.' She'd

63

forgotten her glasses and squinted at the email. 'You'd better read it Mia, we'll be here all day if you wait for me.' She handed the paper to Mia who began to read.

The magpie talisman was an emblem for a club that me and the lads started. We called ourselves 'the Magpie Club' because that's what local folk called us. 'Magpies', because we used to scavenge through the rubbish that was dumped in the brick work's field after the Second World War. Magpies like to steal shiny things, but us boys liked to steal wood for camp fires and broken bits of weaponry and engines disposed of by the American army camp just up the road. It was a great time to be a boy, we'd laze around the bather messing around on a swing made from an old Jeep tyre and a coil of towing rope.'

'Each boy had to make his own magpie talisman and mark it with his initial. We made them from willow because it was easy to carve. We looked out for each other and had a fine, old time.'

'Well that's odd,' said Mia's Nan. She quickly explained what had happened earlier with the key, holding out her hand with the newly found ring glittering on her finger. 'The Magpie Club scavenged for goodies to play with and a real magpie scavenged my key and ring. That's what I call a coincidence!'

'No such thing as coincidence,' said Miss Jaggers. 'This magpie malarkey, well it sounds like the universe is trying to tell you something.' Mia didn't really know what she meant by that, but she did know that what Miss Jaggers' brother had told them was really important. The strange experiences she and Safi had were linked to the boys of the Magpie Club and she had to find out what they meant.

Mia's Nan handed Miss Jaggers a cup of tea. Mia scanned the next paragraph on Miss Jaggers' brother's email. It was something about a recent illness and some hospital tests.

'I'll just pop that away,' said Miss Jaggers reaching for the email, but Bear suddenly came bounding in and knocked her tea out of her hand. Mia's Nan ordered Bear into his bed and fetched kitchen roll and a mop. Miss Jaggers went out to the bathroom to sponge the tea from her pale blue trousers before it stained. Mia peeked at the rest of the letter from

Miss Jaggers' brother. At the bottom was a paragraph that seemed important even though Miss Jaggers had not mentioned it. Mia quickly read...

'It's lovely to remember our fine childhood Sis, we didn't have much money but we were happy. It's been many years since I thought about the old days, my only regret is what happened on the day of poor little Tommy Bassett's death. It's been a burden to me but even now I can't break my promise to the other lads. We'll take the secret to our graves.

Your loving big brother Bernie'

A cold chill ran down Mia's spine. Tommy Bassett had died as a child and there was something about his death that the boys of the Magpie Club wanted to keep secret. So much so that they made a pact with each other to make sure it stayed secret. Mia read it again. Tears pricked at her eyes and her whole body felt frozen to the bone. What happened on the day of Tommy Bassett's death? What promise did the boys make to each other? One way or another Mia knew she had to find out. There was no turning back.

19

Mia was trying to think of a way to ask Miss Jaggers how Tommy Bassett had died but she knew if she brought it up Miss Jaggers would know she had read the rest of the email.

She went upstairs to put on her bed clothes. Downstairs she could hear everyone arriving. Mr and Mrs Jones, Sam and John, Mr Gregory and Mrs Hewitt who investigated people's family trees. Even Robin, the history student from college put in an appearance. Mia was sitting on the top step when her Nan called her to come down to clean her teeth.

She felt embarrassed in her bright pink onesie and scuttled through the history group throng into the kitchen and to the little bathroom beyond. The sun was going down and the room with its small window was shadowy but she didn't turn on the light. She reached for the toothpaste where she knew it would be and squeezed some onto her toothbrush. She turned on the tap then looked in the mirror.

Her own face stared back at her but something was wrong. Mia heard a sound she couldn't identify and then she realised what it was. It was the crackle of frost forming on the mirror filling it bit by bit with spectacular swirls of ice. She wondered at the beautiful patterns whilst being gripped with fear at not understanding what was happening. The sudden drop in temperature turned her skin to goose bumps.

She was suddenly aware of icy breath on the back of her neck and the white vapour of that breath unravelled in the air around her. Her heart raced, thudding against her ribs. And then it happened.

As she looked into the frosty patterns on the mirror she saw that letters were being scratched through the ice and words were being formed before her eyes.

'Ask.' That was the first word. Then 'Mrs Jones.' That was it. 'Ask Mrs Jones.' Mia screwed her eyes shut as tightly as possible, then slowly, very slowly opened them again. The words were gone. She could no longer feel breath on the back of her neck. Stunned and not knowing what to do she attempted to brush her teeth but her hand shook so much she dropped her toothbrush.

Mia looked into the sink. The small pool of water in the bottom of the bowl had turned to ice. She took a big breath and said out loud.

'I'll ask her. I *will* ask her about you Tommy Bassett.'

*   *   *

Mia sat on the edge of the bath and noticed how quickly the temperature went back to normal and how the frost on the mirror seemed to mist over and disappear. She didn't know what to think. Mia was still shaky and put all her effort into trying to calm down. She had to ask Mrs Jones something. What did she have to ask her? What would Mrs Jones know? And then she remembered back to the last history group meeting.

What was it that Mrs Jones had said when everyone was talking about the field at the back of the cottage? It was just before her Nan had caught her sitting at the top of the stairs eavesdropping. Mia tried really hard to remember and then like an electric light going on in her head it suddenly came to her.

When Mia came out of the bathroom Mrs Jones was sorting through a box file of documents on the kitchen counter with Mrs Hewitt. Mia saw her opportunity.

'Mrs Jones, can I ask you something?'

'What is it Mia?' Mrs Jones replied kindly.

'Something you said at the last meeting...about a boy?'

'Oh, I can't remember that far back. What exactly did I say?' By now Mrs Hewitt was also listening to Mia's question.

'Well when everyone was talking about the field at the back and someone said it was a lake and it had been used as a dump, you said something about a boy...'

'Did I?' She thought for a minute. 'Oh yes. There was a boy...He died in the bather.'

'Did he drown?' asked Mia.

'He did. But it was worse than that,' said Mrs Jones.

'How can it be worse than that?' exclaimed Mia.

'Well poor boy went through the ice. Out there on the bather all by himself. Terrible tragedy.' Mia felt weak, her stomach turned over.

'Are you alright Mia?'

'Yes,' she lied, 'do you know anything else?'

'Um, didn't you do some family history on the boy who died in the bather Sylvie?' She turned to Mrs Hewitt.

'Oh, you mean the Bassett boy? Yes. There was a dreadful accident.' She paused as she gathered her thoughts. 'It was Christmas Eve 1950. It was a very cold winter. It snowed for most of December and the snow was a metre deep in places. Everything was frozen, including the bather in the field behind your cottage Mia.

'The poor little lad that died was called Tommy Bassett. He was out on the bather by himself, out on the ice. Goodness knows what possessed him. One minute I suppose he was having fun messing about on the ice the next the ice must have cracked and given way and down he went into the frozen water. Must have been terrifying.' She shook her head sadly. 'No one knew he was missing till that evening and some of his friends said they'd last seen him at the bather. It was dark by then and although they looked for him, he wasn't found.'

'Next morning they went back to look again. It was Christmas day and a group of men from the village came out to the bather. They tied a rope to his dad Stanley and secured it to one of the old willows and he slowly made his way out onto the ice. The men held the rope ready to pull him back if the ice cracked.' She fell silent. In fact there was a hush amongst the whole history group. Everyone was listening to Mrs Hewitt.

'What happened next?' asked Mia.

'He wasn't very steady on his feet, but he was desperate to find his boy. He must have been hoping against hope that he wouldn't find anything out there in the ice. He carefully set out across the solid water, slippery step by slippery step. About a quarter way across he saw it. A line in the ice, like an ancient scar that looked like it had been broken and frozen over again. He knelt down and wiped the film of frost from the icy surface…and that's when he saw him. The face of his boy, his son, staring up through the frozen water, deathly white and motionless. An awful moment caught in time beneath the ice.' Her voice was met by silence.

'I think we need some more shortbread,' said Robin lightening the mood. Everyone seemed to breathe a sigh of relief and carry on doing whatever it was they'd been doing before Mrs Hewitt began speaking.

'What happened next?' Mia asked.

'Well they broke the ice and got him out. Poor lad. Christmas day as well,' she sighed.

'Thanks Mrs Hewitt,' said Mia turning to go.

'There's something else you might find interesting Mia,' said Mrs Hewitt. Mia waited for her to continue. 'Tommy Bassett had a twin brother called Bobby and about ten years ago Bobby's daughter, bearing in mind she's half Canadian, wanted me to research the 'English' side of her family tree. It so happens I showed her this little lane of cottages because this is where the Bassett twins grew up.'

'They lived along here?' asked Mia. She held her breath.

'Down at Bluebell Cottage, by the old plum tree.' Mia let out a sigh of relief. She was glad they hadn't lived in her Nan's cottage. She wanted her Nan's cottage to be filled with happy memories and good times.

'You'll give her nightmares Sylvie,' said Mia's Nan finding the custard creams and adding them to the shortbread. 'Bedtime now Mia, I'll pop up in a minute and tuck you in.' Mia turned to go upstairs and caught Miss Jaggers looking at her. She had been listening to the story Mrs Hewitt had told Mia about Tommy Bassett. Had she guessed that Mia had read the end of her brother's email and his regrets about Tommy Bassett's death?

Mia suddenly remembered that she'd promised to contact Safi.

'Can Safi come over after school tomorrow Nan?' she asked quickly.

'Yes sure, but bed now Mia.'

'Can I just borrow your mobile and ring him, just so his mum knows.' Mia's Nan frowned.

'Alright then, it's in my handbag on my bed.' As Mia walked to the stairs Miss Jaggers grabbed her by the arm.

'Some things are better left alone Mia Page,' she said quietly. Mia's stomach turned. She liked Miss Jaggers but now she felt as if there was something dangerous about finding out about the Magpie Club's secret. She didn't reply, just gently pulled her arm away and went quickly upstairs.

20

Mia lay on her bed looking at the ceiling. She was talking to Safi on her Nan's mobile and waiting for him to digest everything she'd just told him.

'You've had a message from Tommy Bassett? Scratched in ice on the bathroom mirror?' He sounded incredulous.

'Well I think it was him. Who else could it be? I know we're on the right trail Saf. Tommy Bassett drowned in the bather under the ice and Miss Jaggers' brother said his only regret was what happened on the day Tommy Bassett died. He said he'd kept a promise to the other lads but it had been a burden to him. This promise he made, the secret they all kept. We've got to find out what it was.'

'Do you think the boys…' Safi hesitated. 'Do you think the boys killed him? They killed him and then swore to keep it secret?' Mia didn't answer. She felt sick. Safi continued. 'You know what I think? I think the spirit of Tommy Bassett can't rest until that secret's been revealed.'

'But why now? That's what I don't understand. Mrs Hewitt said he died in 1950?'

'Maybe it's only now that all the right circumstances have come together at the same time. Like you moving into the cottage and playing in the back field and finding the magpie token…'

'…and Miss Jaggers and the history group meeting at Nan's house, and Nan working at the old people's home and telling me about Bobby Bassett.'

'I've got an idea,' said Safi. 'Where's the old people's home?'

'At the top of Archibald Crescent opposite the allotments.'

'It would take ten minutes to walk there after school,' said Safi. 'We could go and find Bobby Bassett and see if he can tell us anything about this secret pact.'

'Nan would never let me go off somewhere after school by myself,' said Mia. 'And neither would your mum!'

'Yeah, I suppose you're right. What about asking your Nan to take us after school?'

'She's not going to take us to the old people's home for no reason. We'd have to come up with a really convincing story…' They were silent for a moment, and then with a voice full of excitement Safi exclaimed…

'Got it. We'll tell her the truth!'

'The truth?' said Mia.

'Well it's not every day you see mysterious writing being formed in ice on your bathroom mirror…Or see someone who's been dead for 60 years.'

'I don't know…'

'Even if she doesn't believe that Tommy Bassett is trying to contact us from beyond the grave about some secret pact that was made by the Magpie Club she'll still be curious. She might not believe a ghost is trying to contact us, but she will think something unusual is happening. She'll remember your wet swimsuit and the crying that you heard, we'll show her the magpie tokens. I bet she'll want to get to the bottom of it as much as we do.'

'Maybe,' said Mia.

'We've got to try…'

'Ok, talk to you tomorrow. See ya.'

'Night Mia.'

21

When Mia came downstairs in the morning her Nan was talking on the phone. She smiled at Mia and nodded towards the oven, shaking her finger in the direction of the grill. Mia immediately saw that her pain au chocolat was on the darker side of brown and quickly grabbed a tea towel and pulled out the grill tray. She flipped off the switch and managed to put her breakfast on a plate without burning her fingers.

Sitting at the table she listened to her Nan's call. It was the care home.

'I can't...' said her Nan. 'There's no one to have Mia and besides she's got a friend coming over tonight.' Mia's Nan looked agitated as she listened to what the person on the other end of the phone was saying. 'Even if I could I wouldn't. It's Friday...they've been at school all week, the last thing they'll want to do after school is hang around an old people's home for an hour while I fill in for Mrs Morgan.' Mia's ears pricked up.

'Double time? Do you mean you'll pay me double my normal hourly rate?' There was a pause. Mia stood up and tried to get her Nan's attention.

'Nan...Nan...'

'Hang on a minute, let me have a word with Mia...' She put her hand over the receiver so that whoever she was speaking to couldn't hear what she was saying.

'This is a nightmare Mia, I'm so sorry.' She sighed heavily. 'Mrs Morgan, one of the other care workers at the home is going to be late for her shift this afternoon and with one of the residents poorly they need some extra cover. As we live so close they've asked me to go in for an hour. They'll pay me double the money and don't mind if I bring you and Safi...but, well I've told them I can't drag you along to sit around for an hour while I...'

'Nan, Nan...we don't mind,' Mia interrupted. 'Please say you'll do it. Saf and me will be fine.'

'You're sure?' asked Mia's Nan. Mia nodded.

As she sat down to eat her breakfast she couldn't believe her luck. Everything seemed to be falling into place. They were going to speak to Bobby Bassett at last.

*   *   *

At school that morning Mia couldn't wait to tell Safi about the lucky turn of events. Much to her surprise however Safi came into her class with several other children just before first break. His class were doing a project on advertising and Safi's work group had come to give a presentation on a product they'd invented. More groups from his class would be presenting products they'd invented throughout the day and Mia's class would vote on what product they thought was best. The product that Safi's group were promoting were skateboards for dogs which raised a few smiles even though it was totally impractical.

When they had finished they filed out past Mia's desk. Safi leant over and whispered – 'I've got something really important to show you.' Mia tried to think what it might be. The rest of the lesson dragged by. The hands on the clock hardly seemed to move, but at last the bell rang for break.

Mia didn't have to look far for Safi, he was making his way back to her classroom to find her.

'Let's go somewhere quiet,' he said and began walking back down the corridor. At the stairs he looked around to see if anyone was watching them then quickly ran up the steps. Mia followed him. At the top he turned left and opened the first door on the corridor into a store room. He checked no one was inside and went in. Mia slipped in behind him and closed the door.

'What is it?' she asked, but Safi didn't reply. He walked across the room and sat down in the far corner. Mia followed and sat down next to him. She looked around. Wide shelves were fixed to all the walls and stacked to the ceiling with games and jigsaws, books and craft items. There wasn't a spare surface. 'Why are we here?'

'Because of this.' He reached into his pocket and took something out. He stretched out his hand to Mia and slowly uncurled his fingers. Laying in his palm was a magpie talisman. The roughly carved magpie was face up.

'Did you take one of my tokens?' Mia asked. She was confused, trying to make sense of why Safi would have one of her tokens.

'No, of course not. I found it.'

'What do you mean? Found it?'

'In my pencil case.' Mia thought for a moment.

'Then this is another token. Not one of the ones that came to me.'

'Yes Mia,' Safi said. 'This is another token. The sixth token. I was in class this morning and opened my pencil case and there it was.' Mia looked at Safi.

'Were you ok?'

'I didn't have an asthma attack if that's what you mean.' He gave a choked laugh. 'I think hanging around with a nutter like you helps.' Mia smiled. 'Turn it over.' Mia leaned forward and turned the token over. On the other side was the initial B.

'B...Is that B for Bernard Jaggers or B for Bobby Bassett?'

'Which ever one it is Mia, the appearance of this token means one of them is dead.' Mia felt the blood drain from her face, she pulled her hands to her mouth in horror.

'Nan was talking to the home this morning. She told me one of the residents was ill. What if it was Bobby? If it's Bobby we'll never find out what happened!'

'...and do you remember Miss Jaggers' email from her brother. He said something about having tests at the hospital didn't he? So it could just as easily be Bernard.'

Mia struggled to make sense of her feelings. She didn't want anyone to die. She knew Miss Jaggers would be heartbroken if anything happened to her brother but she also knew Bobby was their only hope of finding out what really happened to Tommy. She remembered what she'd been so excited to tell Safi before school but if Bobby was dead it wouldn't matter anymore.

'Nan has to go to work for an hour when we get home from school. I told her we didn't mind hanging out at the care home. If Bobby's dead, well I suppose that changes everything.' She felt like she was carrying a heavy weight. She stared at the floor and swallowed hard. 'We'll never find out what happened.'

'Hey look, I know this is a horrible situation. Someone's dead and we both wish that wasn't the case. But we've got to carry on. If Bobby has died well we might be able to find out something from your Nan, but actually right now we don't know what has happened.'

'It's too big a coincidence that just when we want to talk to Bobby your Nan has been called into work and has to take us with her. We've got to hope for the best possible outcome Mia. I know it's hard but we just have to wait it out. Agreed?' Mia was silent, her thoughts were dark. 'Mia!'

'Yes, your right. We'll have to wait till after school and then hope we can find out what's happened.'

They got up and made their way to the door. Mia checked that the coast was clear and they quickly left the store room closing the door behind them.

At the top of the stairs there was a large window that looked out onto the playground and as they passed Mia glanced out, observing the children playing games and wandering around arm in arm. Boys were playing football on the field and a group of girls made up dances, but one child caught her attention. He was stood alone in the centre of the playground unmoved by the chaos of running children and the hubbub of shouts and laughter around him. It seemed as if he existed separately. She stared at him, his head was hanging down and he seemed to be a misty grey. He wore shorts and a sleeveless jumper over his shirt, his hair was neatly parted and his boots were made of well-worn leather. She looked more closely. She noticed the wet sheen of his hair, his saturated clothes and the trickle of water that ran

78

down his hand and drip, drip, dripped from his frozen fingers making a small puddle on the playground.

Around him swirled colour and playfulness and childish fun but he stood silent and alone. Then slowly, very slowly he began to lift his head until his eyes met Mia's eyes. It was Tommy Bassett.

'Mia, come on,' snapped Safi, worried they would be caught indoors at break time. Mia looked away for a moment and when she looked back he was gone.

22

The day dragged. Even lunch time which Mia would normally spend talking or playing with Safi was spent showing a new girl called Ellen around the school. Outside the sun was shining but Mia's classroom was hot and stuffy even with all the windows open. The last hour was guided reading and Mia's group sat on the carpet becoming increasingly tired and irritable while they read. When the bell went an overwhelming sense of expectation swept over her. She grabbed her back pack and pushed through the throng of children to Safi's classroom. He met her halfway.

'Nan's going to meet us in the back carpark. She's driving.' Safi nodded and they both made their way out of school. Mia's Nan was already parked and waiting. It was incredibly hot and she'd wound down the windows and was stood by the open door. As they approached she reached into a cool bag on the passenger seat and produced a couple of ice lollies.

'I've got some crisps and biscuits too,' she said as they got in the back of the car. 'Just to tide you over for an hour while we're at the home.'

'Thanks Nan,' said Mia, buckling her seat belt. 'We'll be fine won't we Saf?' Safi was taking the wrapper from his lolly, he locked eyes with Mia and nodded towards her Nan, urging her to ask about Bobby Bassett.

'Um, did you say someone wasn't well this morning Nan?' Mia's Nan started the car.

'Mrs Jefferies. She ate a whole box of chocolates in about 5 minutes flat.' She sighed. 'It messed with her diabetes and made her sick.' Mia and Safi exchanged uneasy glances.

'So Bobby Bassett…the guy who's the boy in that old photo in the field behind our house. It wasn't him them?'

'Oh no, he's fighting fit. Loopy as a nine bob note but ok I think. Why?' Mia didn't say anything for a minute, then asked –

'Miss Jaggers' brother. Bernard. Is he…is he?'

'Is he coming to England to visit his sister this year?' jumped in Safi. Mia's Nan was just pulling into the old people's home.

'Not as far as I know…' She stopped the car and undid her seat belt. Turning round to talk to the children she said. 'I'm only here for an hour to cover for Mrs Morgan. You can sit in the dining room and read or chat or whatever but no shouting and running around. OK?'

They piled out of the car and Mia's Nan led them through a reception area. She keyed a pin code into a pin pad on the wall and the next door opened when she pushed it. She showed them the dining area and they sat down next to each other while Mia's Nan went off to put on her tunic and start work.

Mia and Safi sat at the long dining table listening to Mia's Nan's footsteps receding into the distance. Safi was silently staring at the floor. Waiting. He looked up and met Mia's gaze.

'Ready?' he said.

'As much as I'll ever be.' Mia took a small purse from her back pack and slipped it into her pocket. 'Come on then.'

They went down the corridor in the opposite direction to the one Mia's Nan had taken. The tiled floor was squeaky clean and pictures of bright blossoming flowers hung from the pale blue walls.

There were doors on either side. They were all open and as they walked by Mia and Safi glanced into each room. The elderly occupants were either sleeping, looking out of their windows across the closely cut lawn or sat in high backed armchairs watching TV at an excessively high volume. The children didn't see anyone they thought might be Bobby Bassett.

Ahead of them the corridor came to an end and they could either go right or left.

'Try down here,' Safi indicated to the left. Again there were doors on either side. The first one was slightly ajar and the sound of loud snoring spilled into the corridor. Safi peeped in and stepped back shaking his head. They moved on. The next door was shut. Mia turned the handle and gently pushed the door open.

23

Inside there was a small room. Sunlight flooded through the window. In the corner there was a neatly made bed covered by a red crocheted blanket and next to it a bedside table on which was a lamp, a jug of water, a framed picture and a pair of glasses. There was a chest of drawers in the other corner. On top was a small wooden box and pile of documents weighed down by a heavy snow globe. Within the globe was the model of a willow tree with heavy branches. An arm chair had been drawn close to an open patio door and although the chair was facing away from them they could see that there was someone sat in it. Just outside there was a bird table on which was a lone magpie, the sound of its familiar 'chakka chakka' chatter drifted into the room.

Mia and Safi tentatively walked in and closed the door behind them.

'Mr Bassett? Mr Bassett?' Mia enquired. There was no answer. They approached the chair.

'Beautiful. Isn't it?' a frail voice said. Mia walked forward and looked out into the garden.

'The magpie? Yes. I love that bluey black colour and the long tail feathers.'

'...they're clever little buggers,' he added. Mia turned and looked at the man.

'Are you Bobby Bassett?' The man didn't take his eyes off of the magpie on the bird table.

'They call me Robert these days. That's what it says on all the forms. My friends used to call me Bobby...and my brother...my brother used to call me Bob.'

'You mean your brother Tommy?' asked Safi moving closer.

'My brother Tommy....'

Bobby Bassett was a thin, small man and the large chair seemed to swallow him up. His face was long and deeply creased and there were heavy, dark rings under his piercing blue eyes. He had a good head of short, grey hair and wore a long sleeved blue cotton shirt and a pair of neatly pressed trousers. On his feet were tartan slippers.

'Hello Bobby, my name's Mia. I live in one of the cottages near the bather. Just a few doors away from where you lived when you were a boy.' Bobby was silent for a moment, taking in what Mia had said.

'The bather's gone. The bather's not there anymore.'

'It has gone now. The bather's not there anymore Bobby, but look what we found. Look what we found just where the bather used to be.' Mia rummaged in her purse looking for something specific. 'Look,' she moved forward and held out one of the magpie tokens for him to see.

At first Bobby ignored her. He looked straight ahead into the garden, but eventually his eyes turned to the token. He looked more closely.

Suddenly he took it from her and gasped – *'Get my glasses, get my glasses.'* Safi saw some glasses on the bedside table, fetched them and gave them to the Bobby. He clumsily pushed on the spectacles then held the magpie talisman close to his eyes to examine it.

He looked at the roughly carved magpie then turning it over traced his finger over the letter T scratched on the back.

'The magpie was Colin's idea.' His feeble voice was shaking. *'If we're calling ourselves the Magpie Club then we should have a magpie on our membership token'*, - that's what Colin said.' He smiled to himself. 'Den and Bernie had penknives and we had to take turns to use them. I think Den did most of the magpies, he was good at that sort of thing, but we carved our own initials.' He gently stroked the initial T on the token he was holding. His eyes became watery. 'This is Tommy's token...' his voice became unsteady, his words disjointed. 'My....brother...he wasn't a bad lad...if only....if only...' Mia noticed a tear running down his cheek.

'If only what?' she asked. Bobby's face crumpled up, holding back the tears. 'If only what?' Mia insisted... 'if only what?' Bobby turned to her, he sighed deeply.

'If only he hadn't played those silly games…silly, silly games he played…trying to fool us into believing…he'd be alive now. With me…he'd have had a life….oh Tommy. Silly games…'

'What silly games?' Safi asked. Bobby held his hands to his head. His words were desperate and disordered. 'I can't tell…no, no. I can't, I made a vow not to tell.' He sounded choked as tears caught in his throat. 'We all did. We all made a promise to each other.'

'What promise?' asked Mia.

'I can't say…we promised we wouldn't tell anyone what happened.' Another tear ran down his cheek. 'We promised.' He sounded hysterical and began to sob.

Just as Mia was bending down to Bobby the door opened and Mia's Nan stood there looking stunned and puzzled.

'What's going on? What are you two doing here?'

'Nan. We had to talk to Bobby.' Mia's Nan walked into the room.

'Is this about that stupid photograph?' She turned to Bobby. 'I'm sorry Mr Bassett, this is my granddaughter Mia and her friend Safi. They're trying to find out about a photograph she found of you and some boys in the field at the back of our cottage.' She put her arm around Bobby to comfort him. 'They shouldn't have come in here. I didn't know. I'm so sorry my love.' She threw a dark look at Mia. 'You should know better young lady. Go back to the dining room and don't let me hear another peep out of the pair of you.' And then as if to make her point absolutely clear she added. 'I'm very disappointed in you Mia.'

Mia and Safi began to walk to the door, they looked at each other in desperation. This had been their only chance to speak to Bobby Bassett and they'd blown it. Safi hesitated then stopped.

'Mrs Page, we're sorry. But, well…it's not just the photo…there are other things…things we can't explain. Things we're trying to find the answer to. Bobby, he's the only one who knows. He's the only one who can help us.'

'What are you talking about?' Bobby stopped crying and Mia's Nan placed a protective hand on his shoulder.

'There's a mystery surrounding Bobby's brother's death,' said Mia. 'Something that no one knew about except the boys in the Magpie Club. Something that hasn't been spoken of for over 60 years.' Mia's Nan was confused.

'Mia, a little boy died a long time ago. He drowned after the ice he was playing on broke. It's very sad, but it was an accident. You coming here bringing it up after all these years… it will only cause upset and pain to Mr Bassett.'

'But he knows what happened.'

'Mia!' her Nan spoke sharply. 'Stop it now.'

'Mrs Page, please believe us. The boys from the Magpie Club know what happened. They made a vow never to tell anyone but it's time to find out.'

'Look Safi, I know how persuasive Mia can be. You don't have to get pulled into all of this.' She turned to Mia, 'Your imagination's got the better of you young lady. There is no mystery.' Mia took out her purse.

'He's not getting pulled into anything Nan. I'm not imagining anything and I can prove it. Ask Bobby about these.' Mia emptied the tokens onto the bed.

'What's that?' Asked Mia's Nan walking over to look at them.

'These appeared one day in my bedroom. They belong to the boys of the Magpie Club, the boys in the photo. Bobby's holding the one that Bear found by the bather, that's his brother's - Tommy's! Each token has an initial on the back and each token belongs to a boy that is now dead. A boy that no longer has to keep the secret.' Mia's Nan looked shocked. Bobby stood up and shuffled towards the bed, Mia's Nan helped him sit down on the crocheted quilt. He picked the tokens up to look at them one by one.

'This doesn't prove anything Mia.'

'There have been so many things Nan that made no sense by themselves. The crying in the night, my wet swimming costume, the magpies, the boy in the mist on the field, the writing on the mirror. There's been so much I haven't told you.'

'I'm still waiting for you to prove something to me,' said Mia's Nan.

'Just ask Bobby, he'll tell you.'

'Mr Bassett is in no fit state to be trying to remember such upsetting things.'

Bobby suddenly spoke...

'Where's Bernie's token? Is Bernie still with us? Is he still keeping the secret?'

'Well, thank goodness, some common sense at last. This secret you keep on going on about...well Bernie Jaggers is still alive, let's ask him about it.' Bobby looked aghast. But it was Safi who spoke.

'Today I found this in my pencil case.' He pulled the magpie token from his pocket. Mia's Nan took it and looked at both sides.

'So you're telling me this B scratched on the back is for Bernard? You're telling me that Bernard is dead?'

'We don't know Nan, but Bobby is alive and the only other person it could be with the initial B is... Bernard.'

24

Mia and Safi were left in the dining room while Mia's Nan
went to call Miss Jaggers. If Bernard Jaggers was dead it
would explain the appearance of the token in Safi's pencil
case. A few minutes later Mia's Nan returned. All the colour
had drained from her face. She looked at them.

'It's true. Bernie died in his sleep. He hadn't been well for
a while. Mary's beside herself.' She pressed her lips together
hardly daring to speak. 'That means Bobby is the only
member of the Magpie Club still alive.' She looked from Mia
to Safi. 'What now?'

'If we want all these strange things to stop we have to
know what happened on the day Tommy Bassett died,' said
Safi. Mia's Nan nodded.

'Come on then.' She turned round and headed for Bobby's
room. Mia and Safi followed.

Mia's Nan opened the door to Bobby's room but it was
empty. They checked the en suite and the built in wardrobe.
The patio windows were still open wide but Bobby was
nowhere to be found.

'Look,' said Safi. He pointed to the bed. 'The magpie
tokens are gone.'

'So is his cap. Bobby doesn't go anywhere unless he's
wearing his cap,' Mia's Nan sighed and wearily put her hand
to her head. 'That means he's left the home. I'm only here an
hour and I've gone and lost someone.'

'I think I know where he'll be heading,' said Mia. She and
Safi looked at each other and said together –

'…the bather.'

'Right, my shift's just ending. I'll let someone know what's
happened and we'll go and look for him. Here, meet me by
the car, I'll be out in a minute.' She handed Mia her car keys
and disappeared. Mia and Safi collected their back packs from
the dining room and went out to the car.

They were strapped in ready to go a few minutes later

when Mia's Nan opened the car door.

'Matron's called the police. They're sending out some special constables to drive around the area and try to spot him.' She started the car and drove onto the road.

'Did you tell them where we think he's going?' asked Mia.

'I've just lost one of our residents Mia, I'm not going to make matters worse by telling her about the bather, the Magpie Club and disembodied crying in the night!'

They drove across the roundabout and onto the main road out of the village. On one side there was a patchwork of fields and on the other an estate of large detached houses which gave way to a small row of red brick Victorian terraces.

'There he is!' exclaimed Safi. They watched Bobby disappear down a small track on the left between the houses.

'He's going across the park to the bather,' said Mia.

'We'll be home in a minute. If he's heading to the bather we'll find him,' said Mia's Nan. She indicated left and they turned into a narrow lane. The car bumped along a rutted path. Mia's Nan parked under a walnut tree by the edge of the back field. They quickly got out and ran past the hazel bushes. Bobby had to be found.

25

Mia and Safi saw him first by the half open gate to the field. They stopped and waited for Mia's Nan and then together they slowly walked forward and stood either side of him. He was staring ahead, his face not portraying his thoughts.

It was a hot afternoon and the heat made the air quiver. Hazy, sparkling light shivered above the long grass. Swallows crisscrossed the bright blue sky and dragonflies, their transparent wings traced with turquois, weaved through the dry nettle heads. But it was the sawing hum of the crickets which made their heads whirl as the sun blazed down. Then Bobby spoke.

'There's always been crickets here. When we were boys we used to catch them and keep them in jars. Tommy had a cricket 5 inches long. No word of a lie.'

'You must have lots of memories,' said Mia's Nan. There was silence for a minute and then Bobby said.

'We had some good times here...before...'

'Before what?' asked Mia. Bobby sighed and closed his eyes.

'Before Tommy died.'

'What happened Bobby?' asked Safi. 'What happened when Tommy died?'

'We made a vow. Bernie said if we told anyone they'd blame us...'

'There's only you now Bobby,' said Mia. 'The other boys are dead. You can tell us now. It's ok. It doesn't have to be a secret anymore.' The hum of the crickets seemed to get louder. After a while Bobby spoke.

'Seven for a secret never to be told...there were seven boys in the Magpie Club until Tommy...until Tommy died. Seven for a secret never to be told....that's what Bernie said.'

'Bernie's not here now,' said Safi. Bobby dropped his head and out spilled the words like a magic spell tumbling into the world...the truth that had been kept secret for so long.

'Tommy liked to pretend…one time he pretended he'd found a dead mermaid in the stream and we traipsed across the fields full of excitement to find some odd thing he'd made with Bernie's sister's dolly. He thought it was funny.' Bobby smiled to himself. 'That was our Tommy. Always trying to make you believe something that wasn't true – it got him into a few punch ups too when his shenanigans upset the wrong people.'

'What happened on the day he died?' asked Mia. Bobby looked over to the willow copse, the branches arced like a loose curtain of pale green leaves.

'It was a bitter cold day. We were all there. The bather was iced over and we were sliding around in our boots playing some Russian spy game. It was Christmas Eve. I was excited. I was going to get a crystal set. We'd been there all afternoon and the last bit of sun was disappearing. We were cold and wet and a few flakes of snow were falling. It was time to head home but Tommy…Tommy wanted to carry on playing. He didn't like it when we said we were going.'

'The rest of us began walking back across the field. The snow was getting heavier, it was going to be a white Christmas. We were laughing and messing around. That was the last time I was truly happy.' He took a deep breath. 'Then we heard Tommy shouting. We couldn't see him, it was almost dark and the snow was becoming a blizzard. He was calling *Help me, help me*' – that was the kind of thing Tommy would do. We thought we knew what would happen if we ran back…Tommy would jump out from behind a tree with that big grin on his face saying, '*I was only joking…*' He wanted to play on the ice in the dark and we didn't. It was that simple.' Tears ran down his face and his voice cracked as he spoke. 'So we carried on walking away. We walked away while my brother drowned.'

Mia's Nan put her arm around his shoulder.

'You were children Bobby. You weren't to blame…'

They looked out onto the field, golden headed ragwort leaned into clumps of brown grass and fat bees sat in the whiskery petals of purple thistles.

'What's that?' said Mia as she pointed to a white fleck floating through the air. She let it settle on her hand. Her voice shook as she said. 'It's a snowflake.' Then there was another and another until the air was filled with falling flakes of snow.

'What's going on Nan?' asked Mia. She began to feel frightened.

'I…I don't know love.' A mist was beginning to fall and the sun became an indistinct silvery disc. Mia felt goose bumps on her arms as the temperature dropped.

'Nan, Saf, Look at our breath.' It was suddenly so cold that their breath was white. They all stared into the field where the sound of cracking and crunching was getting closer and closer until at last they saw what it was; a carpet of frost creeping across the ground towards them. It stopped abruptly at the gate. Mia breathed in deeply, the cold air scratched her throat. The birds and crickets fell silent and an eerie stillness descended.

Out of nowhere a boy's voice could be heard. His words sent shivers down Mia's spine.

'*Help me, help me.*'

Bobby gripped the gate, his knuckles were white.

'Nan, I'm scared.' She shivered involuntarily. Safi reached for her hand.

'It's alright Mia.'

'Look,' said Mia's Nan. 'Look.' All four of them stared into the frozen mist and there in the distance they could just make out movement. Then Bobby realised what was happening before all of them and let out a cry of pain and relief, joy and sorrow all mixed into one.

In the field, half blurred by the mist but still identifiable were the boys. The boys of the Magpie Club. The dead boys. Dennis Gregory with his neatly parted hair, Bernard Jaggers in his tightly buttoned jacket, Paul Marshall, Colin Keyes and Gerald Manders. The ghosts of the boys of the Magpie Club.

They stood for a while, faint images in the mist until the

silence was interrupted again…

'*Help me, help me.*' It was a boy's voice emanating from the willows.

'That's Tommy…that's our Tommy,' cried Bobby. As he spoke the boys in the mist began to beckon him, their ghostly voices calling his name. 'I've got to go.' He stumbled over his words. 'I can't let him down this time. He's giving me a second chance. He's giving us all a second chance.' He walked unsteadily through the open gate. Mia's Nan caught his shoulder.

'Are you sure Bobby?' He nodded emphatically. Then with renewed vigour he turned to Mia and Safi.

'Thank you. If it wasn't for you I might never have got this chance. I hope it's not too late.' As he finished speaking another heartfelt '*help me*' penetrated the mist and swirling snow. The ghostly forms of the boys from the Magpie Club beckoned and called out for Bobby to join them.

Bobby walked forward and in moments disappeared into the mist. After years of bearing the burden of the secret alone he was at last in the company of friends. He was with the Magpie Club again.

26

To Mia it seemed like minutes before anything happened but it could have been seconds. She blinked away a snowflake and the mist began to rise. At the same time the frosty grass began to recede and instead of snowflakes a flurry of white dandelion seeds twirled about pushed by a light, warm breeze. The sun became too bright to look at. The field was visible again in all its beauty and the sawing hum of the crickets and melodic song of the sky larks filled the air.

Mia and Safi looked around anxiously.

'Nan, where's Bobby?' Mia's Nan had already started to walk into the field.

'I'm hoping he's at the bather.' She started to run across the field. Mia and Safi overtook her and ran ahead.

At the willow copse Mia could see Bobby sat on the ground. He was leant against a tree stump and had his back to them. He wasn't moving. Mia and Safi ran down the slope and cautiously approached the old man.

'Don't just stand there, come and give me a hand.' Mia and Safi rushed forward.

'You're OK,' Mia cried with relief. Safi and Mia pulled him to his feet. Mia's Nan arrived and rushed over to help them.

'Oh thank goodness. You had us worried there for a minute.' Bobby took some deep breaths and shook his head in disbelief.

'I never thought the day would come…I…I' He held on to Mia's Nan. 'I'm feeling a bit giddy Mrs Page.'

'Well I'm not surprised. I'll tell you what let's sit you down again and call an ambulance. Have a proper ride back to the home. All the other old folk will be looking out of their windows saying *'that Mr Bassett only went and did a runner and they've brought him back in an ambulance.'* They'll be talking about you for weeks.' They carefully helped Bobby sit down again.

'Mia, Safi, you stay here with Bobby. I've left my phone in the car, I'll be back in a minute.' And she was gone.

Mia and Safi sat down next to Bobby.

'Did you kids put those stones around the edge of the bather?' Safi nodded.

'That's when we found Tommy's magpie token.'

'Tommy likes those stones. Says it makes the place special.'

'What was Tommy like?' asked Mia.

'Well, do you know the story of the boy who cried wolf?' They nodded. 'That was our Tommy...he just cried wolf one time too many.'

'Did he leave the tokens in my bedroom and in Saf's pencil case? Only I thought I saw him, in the storm, here in the field the night I found them.' Bobby nodded gently.

'And...' Safi hesitated. '...and...why did he come back?'

'To give me a chance to put things right...He knows how sorry I am. But it gave him a chance to put things right too. He was sorry for what he did. That's why he couldn't rest,' he sighed. 'That's enough. No more talking about this. Let this have peace now.' Safi nodded.

'I just have one more thing to ask,' said Mia. Bobby gave her a look of resignation. 'I kept hearing a child crying in the night. I was wondering...Was that you? Crying for your brother and the terrible secret you had to keep? Almost as if the horror of what had happened captured your sobbing in the very air around the bather.' Bobby looked down and slowly nodded.

'I cried a lot of tears. But that's over now. Let this be the end of it.' Mia and Safi silently acknowledged his words. Mia noticed how the stones they'd placed around the bather gleamed in the sun as if newly washed.

'What was it like here when you were growing up Bobby?' asked Safi.

'Oh...we didn't have a care in the world. There was a rail line with an old skip thing on it from when this was a brick works and we used to get in it and bang along the track and prise open canisters dumped by the Americans during the war filled with petroleum and God knows what else. Truth is we could have killed ourselves a dozen different ways…' Bobby told them about his childhood, the first time he'd talked about it since he'd been a child and Mia and Safi sat and listened to the stories until the ambulance came.

That evening Mia sat in the garden with her Nan and Safi as the copper burnished sun melted into a dazzling red and orange horizon. A magpie landed on the roof of the shed, shattering the peace with its noisy chatter. They watched as it preened and strutted for a moment and then swooping down from the tree a second magpie joined it. The playful 'chakka chakka' chatter of the magpies made Mia smile. She looked at her Nan.

'Two for joy,' she said.

Epilogue

Bobby Bassett recovered well after his strange experience at the bather and became good friends with Miss Jaggers. Mia's Nan invited them for dinner several times and Bobby entertained them with stories about the mischief he and Bernard got up to when they were boys.

The only mystery left was the disappearance of the magpie tokens. Bobby had taken them with him the afternoon he'd gone to the bather but he had no idea what happened to them. The only one left was his own and he gave it to the children as a keepsake.

As for Mia and Safi they didn't spend much time together during the summer because Mia's mum took some leave from the army and she and Mia went to Greece to splash about in the sea and build sandcastles. Safi went to stay with his aunty in Cornwall and did the same thing. But as the holidays came to an end Mia's mum had to go back to the army and Safi returned from Cornwall.

A few days before the new term started Safi and his mum visited Mia and her Nan.

'Thanks for coming round,' Mia said.

'My mum brought your Nan some beans from our allotment.'

'Yum….' said Mia pulling a face to show she didn't mean 'yum' at all.

'Better than eggs!' said Safi. Mia noticed a letter in his hand but before she could say anything Safi asked.

'Did you see Warriors of Albion this week?'

'YES…I bet you loved the magical battle between the witch of Sardeeni and the Black Queen?' Mia was getting excited and they both said together…

'THAT CROWN!'

'All those amazing jewels and the golden flowers. Wow. Just wow. Wouldn't you love one just like it?'

'It's a bit girly for me,' said Safi.

'It was fabulous. I thought it would fall off the Black Queen's head it was so big. I wonder how she kept it on.'

'Well...' said Safi no longer able to contain himself. He flourished the letter he'd been holding. 'We could always ask her?' Mia was puzzled.

'What do you mean?'

'Do you remember me telling you about a competition I was going to enter to win a day on the Warriors of Albion film set?' Realisation dawned on Mia.

'You mean...you mean...'

'Yes. I won!' he screamed with excitement. 'We're going to the studio to watch them film a scene for the next series, we're going to have lunch with the cast and stay in a posh hotel....' They held onto each other's shoulders screeching and laughing and jumping up and down.

'Let's tell Nan.' Mia grabbed Safi's arm and dragged him into the garden.

Darkness was falling quickly and the sawing hum of the crickets filled the air. There were no more secrets and the future was just around the corner waiting for two excited and noisy children to jump into it.

THE END

About the Author

Joy McNally-Bells' debut novel was inspired by her
granddaughter's love of spooky stories.

Joy writes articles and blogs on a variety of subjects. She has
recently turned her hand to researching local ghost stories,
hosting ghost walks and reading tarot cards, so the jump to
telling ghostly tales was perhaps inevitable.

Joy studied Literature and the History of Ideas at Bradford
University. She has two grown up children and of course an
inspirational granddaughter. Joy lives with a large labradoodle
called Sparky in a cottage that backs onto an overgrown field.
She is currently working on a new story about werewolves.